"If I kiss you, I probably won't like it."

Suz winked. "And then what motivation do I have to win the race? I'd just toss you back into the pond for Daisy."

Cisco drew back, startled. "That wouldn't be good."

Suz nodded. "It could be horrible. You could be a wet kisser. Eww."

"I really don't think I am." His ego took a small dent.

"You could be a licky kisser."

"Pretty sure I'm just right, like Goldilock's bed," he said, his ego somewhere down around his boots and flailing like a leaf on the ground in the breeze.

"I don't know," Suz said thoughtfully. "Friends don't let friends kiss friends."

"I'm not that good of a friend."

"You really want a kiss, don't you?"

He perked up at these heartening words that seemed to portend a softening in her stance. "I sure do."

"Hope you get someone to kiss you one day, then. See you around, Cisco."

Dear Reader,

Our visit to Bridesmaids Creek continues! In
The Twins' Rodeo Rider, Cisco Grant (Frog to his
fellow SEALs) is determined to win Suz Hawthorne,
but the town's magic seems determined to pair him
with wild child Daisy Donovan. Yet Suz is just far too
tempting for this red-blooded cowboy, and there's
not enough magic in the world to convince him that
his heart should feel otherwise. In the small town
that was made for matchmaking, there's always
a few turns on the journey to love—which Cisco
learns along the way!

I hope you enjoy Suz and Cisco's story, and I
hope you'll plan on visiting for the last book in the
Bridesmaids Creek series, *The Cowboy SEAL's
Triplets.*

Best wishes always,

Tina Leonard

THE TWINS'
RODEO RIDER

———

TINA LEONARD

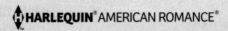

HARLEQUIN® AMERICAN ROMANCE®

Recycling programs
for this product may
not exist in your area.

ISBN-13: 978-0-373-75554-7

The Twins' Rodeo Rider

Copyright © 2015 by Tina Leonard

Printed in U.S.A.

www.Harlequin.com

Tina Leonard is a *USA TODAY* bestselling and award-winning author of more than fifty projects, including several popular miniseries for the Harlequin American Romance line. Known for bad-boy heroes and smart, adventurous heroines, her books have made the *USA TODAY*, Waldenbooks, Ingram and Nielsen BookScan bestseller lists. Born on a military base, Tina lived in many states before eventually marrying the boy who did her crayon printing for her in the first grade. You can visit her at tinaleonard.com, and follow her on Facebook and Twitter.

Books by Tina Leonard

Harlequin American Romance

Bridesmaids Creek

THE REBEL COWBOY'S QUADRUPLETS
THE SEAL'S HOLIDAY BABIES

Callahan Cowboys

A CALLAHAN WEDDING
THE RENEGADE COWBOY RETURNS
THE COWBOY SOLDIER'S SONS
CHRISTMAS IN TEXAS
"Christmas Baby Blessings"
A CALLAHAN OUTLAW'S TWINS
HIS CALLAHAN BRIDE'S BABY
BRANDED BY A CALLAHAN
CALLAHAN COWBOY TRIPLETS
A CALLAHAN CHRISTMAS MIRACLE
HER CALLAHAN FAMILY MAN
SWEET CALLAHAN HOMECOMING

Visit the Author Profile page
at Harlequin.com for more titles.

Many thanks to the many wonderful readers who so faithfully support my work. I appreciate you more than I can ever say!

Chapter One

Francisco Rodriguez Olivier Grant stared at the very petite, very darling woman dressing him down. Suz Hawthorne giving a man hell was an impressive sight despite
her five foot two and a half inch size, due to the streaky
blue-in-blond hair, strategically placed cheek studs, a
tiny diamond stud in her nose and a miniscule silver
loop in her right eyebrow. Though they were small and
delicately designed, her tats spoke loudly of her rebel
status—a fragile red rose on one wrist, and a beautiful,
delicate Celtic cross on the other. When a man adored
a woman like he adored Suz, being in her line of fire
was enough to nail a man's boots to the ground—and
his boots were nailed down good.

"Here's the deal, so pay attention." Suz put her hands
on her rounded, feminine hips, guiding his eyes farther
down her oh-so-delicious body. Well, he just knew her
body would feel delicious—if he could get his hands
on it.

"I'm paying *close* attention."

"All right. I can't bring myself to call you Frog like
everybody else does. I've never seen a man look less
frog-like or toadly in my life. There's nothing amphibi-
ous about you, beyond your ability to swim."

He started to say, "I don't care what you call me as long as you call me," then realized that would sound desperate. Or something. "Thanks."

"Good. I'm glad that's settled."

Suz's brain was a wonder to contemplate, and right now, operating about two gears faster than his. Mainly because he was sidelined by what he belatedly recognized as surefire, 100 percent lust. "What's settled?"

"Your name."

He grinned at the sweet-'n'-sassy bombshell, who was disarming him completely. "You're going to call me Francisco Rodriguez Olivier Grant every time you speak to me?"

"No. From now on, you're just Cisco."

He took that in.

"Perhaps your silence means you're not crazy about that. But Frog just isn't working for me."

"Fine. I don't care. Address me as Santa Claus if you want." He got his swagger back and then some, kind of impressed that she wanted to call him Cisco. There were probably any number of legendary hanging, swinging badasses that had been called Cisco over time.

Not so many named Frog. He'd been named Frog courtesy of his SEAL brothers, because he could out-swim just about every man around.

"Frog" was fine under certain conditions. But when a man wanted a woman thinking about him—and a dynamite package like Suz most particularly—it was probably better to be a Cisco.

"Now that we have that settled, you're going to escort me to the upcoming Bridesmaids Creek swim."

"The newly christened Cisco feels like he's missing a bit of info. We just had a swim for Jade Harper and Ty

Spurlock, which is why they're married, according to the tenets of the fabled charm, right? As I recall, I swam that race pretty quickly." And he was none too pleased, because the way the rumor mill worked in Bridesmaids Creek, the prize for winning the swim was the woman waiting on the banks at the finish line.

The woman at the finish line that day had been Daisy Donovan, and a more annoying wild woman he'd never had the bad luck to come across.

He wanted Suz. Not Daisy.

But supposedly the legend, charm, magic—whatever you wanted to call it—of Bridesmaids Creek had never, ever misfired. Daisy definitely thought she was his— and was convinced enough of that fact that lately he'd been considering taking himself to parts very far away from the small, family-centered town.

"Yes, your swim was impressive. But another one is scheduled. I've decided to challenge Daisy for you."

This was news he could use. "Really?"

Suz nodded. "Yes."

"Does the charm work that way?" He scarcely dared to hope.

"We don't know. In your case, we're calling it an evil spell. You might say we're messing with our own potion here in BC." Suz looked thoughtful. "It's very experimental. Frankly, we don't know what could happen if we sidestep the legend."

"Well, I won't be going off with Daisy," he said cheerfully.

"Or you could fall head over heels in love with her. As I mentioned, we've never tinkered with our town mysteries before."

He felt some hope. "So, you want to win me, huh?"

He resisted the urge to stick out his chest, show off his pecs, showcase himself a little.

"Not really, but I drew short straw." Suz got into her truck, completely unaware she'd just flattened his ego. "Ladies don't swim the race. It's the man's job to win his female. Or so we've always assumed. It's been this way dating back to the early days of Bridesmaids Creek."

He gulped. "You mean *I'll* be standing on the banks waiting for the winner to win me?"

"Exactly."

That scared the hell out of him. Suz was diminutive, while Daisy was more…well, Daisy was mean and beautiful and hotheaded. Looked pretty athletic, too, as she raced up and down the main drag on her motorcycle.

"Can't I just say I don't believe in voodoo and ghosts and crap, and it'll blow over?" The thought gave him hope. "I could just ignore it and it might go away. Or Daisy might find another guy."

"She's got her sights set right on you. And just so you know, we don't do voodoo in BC. We have magic." Suz started the engine. "I learned to swim in the sixth grade, and though I really haven't done more than dog-paddle in years, it's got to be like falling off a bike, right?"

Oh, boy. "Cisco" smiled, felt a bit pained and wondered how he'd come to land in a town that was, as his friend Ty said—that same Ty who'd convinced him to come to Bridesmaids Creek—a town full of carneys and soothsayers all selling the BC shtick.

Yet if he hadn't come to BC to help the locals breathe new life into BC, he would have never met the amazing, gifted, full-lipped, daunting Suz Hawthorne. And that would've been a shame. Even if she didn't seem to reciprocate his feelings, he was certain this radioactive doll had his name all over her. Reserved *especially* for him. "Do me a favor. Since I'm agreeing to escort you."

"Name it."

"Kiss me." He leaned close to the window to give her prime access.

"Why would I want to do that?" Suz's blue eyes widened.

"Because I have nice lips. Or so I've been told. Pucker up, dollface."

"I don't pucker for anyone who calls me 'dollface,' unless you want me to look like I bit into a grapefruit. Now *that* kind of pucker may be available to you."

He laughed. "So much sass, so little honesty."

She sniffed. "I'm trying to *save* you, cowboy, not romance you. Don't confuse this."

"No kiss? I really feel like I need to know if you're the woman of my dreams, if you're determined to win me. And a kiss tells all."

"Oh, wow." Suz looked incredulous. "You really let that line out of your mouth?"

"Slid out easily. Come on, cupcake." He closed some distance between her face and his in case she changed her mind. *Strike while the branding iron was hot* was a very worthwhile strategy. It was in fact his favorite strategy.

"If I kiss you, I probably won't like it. And then what motivation do I have to win the race? I'd just toss you back into the pond for Daisy."

He drew back, startled. "That wouldn't be good."

Suz nodded. "It could be horrible. You could be a wet kisser. Eww."

"I really don't think I am." His ego took a small dent.

"You could be a licky-kisser."

"Pretty sure I'm just right, like Goldilock's bed," he

said, his ego somewhere down around his boots and flailing like a leaf in the breeze.

"I don't know," Suz said thoughtfully. "Friends don't let friends kiss friends."

"I'm not *that* good of a friend."

"You really want a kiss, don't you?"

He perked up at these heartening words that seemed to portend a softening in her stance. "I sure do."

"Hope you get someone to kiss you one day, then. See you around, Cisco. And don't forget, one week until the swim!"

"Hey!" He stopped her from driving off. "How am I supposed to get you in shape in a week?"

Suz raised a brow. "In shape for what?"

"Winning me?"

She winked. "I'm off to The Wedding Diner to eat a piece of four-layer chocolate cake Jane Chatham promised to hold back for me. I guess you'll have to cross today off your list for training."

She drove away, her angelic smile doing nothing to ease his trauma. Suz wasn't trying very hard, as far as he could tell. Somehow she'd gotten roped into this race—*short straw indeed*—and obviously had no plans to seriously go for the win.

Which meant his Daisy problem was still alive and well. Frog—no, Cisco, because that's who Suz decreed he was, and he was fine with whatever she wanted—decided he was going to have to make sure that he was absolutely, 100 percent, the gold buckle of bachelors she just couldn't live without winning.

Cisco was busily plotting how to best tempt Suz into putting some real effort into winning him—as much effort as she'd put into going off for chocolate cake—when the familiar roar of Daisy Donovan's motorcycle disrupted him. The siren brunette with long chocolate locks pulled up beside him and slipped off her helmet. Daisy was a heart attack on wheels and she knew it. The thing was, she had a very dark side, courtesy of her old man, Robert Donovan, who'd haunted this town for years trying to run it into the ground so he could take over the real estate.

Ty Spurlock had brought Cisco, Justin Morant, Squint Mathison and Sam Barr to town on a bride hunt, to help repopulate the town and fortify it against Robert's manipulations. Justin had fallen first, for Mackenzie Hawthorne, becoming a father to her four darling quadruplet sweethearts. Then Ty had fallen into his own trap—and no one much saw him these days between his deployments and loving on Jade Harper Spurlock and their twin tiny dolls.

The real kicker was that their buddy Squint had a thing for Daisy. He was just positive her brand of wild child needed him for taming. For some reason, Daisy never looked his way. She preferred instead to cast her lure for a frog—well, a Cisco. He looked at the long-legged brunette with the sexy-devil smile cautiously.

"Hi, Daisy."

"Hello, lover boy."

He winced. "Nice January day, huh?"

Daisy laughed. "You're cute when you're nervous."

"I'm not nervous." He drew himself up. A navy SEAL did not get nervous over brunettes who ripped up the road on motorcycles and tried to tie you down.

Okay, maybe a little nervous. Just because of the tying down thing.

"If you're not nervous, kiss me."

She gave him a sultry look that singed his toes. He felt his boots smoking. "I'd better not. It's probably bad luck to kiss before the big swim," he said.

"If you don't want to get lucky, fine by me."

His throat dried out. He could practically feel sweat pouring out from underneath his hat, when it was a perfectly frigid twenty degrees Fahrenheit outside. "I'm late to meet Squint and Sam. See you, Daisy."

"Hey."

He stopped and, looking at her, his heart wadded into a knot. "Yes?"

"If you change your mind about getting lucky, I'll be around."

He tipped his hat, hurried off. Her motorcycle roared, and she headed in the opposite direction. Relief ran all over him as he went to find Sam and Squint.

His buddies were parked in Sheriff Dennis McAdams's office, kicking back, having a good jaw with the sheriff. Sam and Dennis grinned hugely at him, while Squint glared.

"We saw you accosting Daisy out there," Sam said. "Squint's jealous."

"Yeah, that's what I was doing." Cisco tossed himself into a chair. "Did you also see me chatting up Suz?"

"No, we didn't see that." Dennis looked pleased, lounging behind his wide wood desk that had seen many, many years of boot heels resting on it. "Well, we might have seen you trying to get very close to our Suz, but from here, it looked to us like she backed away in a hurry. A real, real hurry."

The men laughed—except for Squint. "Hey, brother,"

Cisco said, "if you want Daisy so badly, please take her off my hands. By all means."

That would allow him to concentrate on Suz, which was his preeminent goal.

Squint frowned. "She seems to prefer Frog legs."

Frog legs, nothing! He held up a hand. "Cisco is the name, boys."

"Since when?" Dennis palmed through some papers. "I don't have any paperwork here stating such."

"Can't a man change his name because a beautiful woman wants him to?" Cisco was pretty proud to brag on the fact that he alone had been newly anointed by one of the town's most awesome, sexy bachelorettes.

"Daisy?" Squint glared some more. "Daisy wants you to go by Cisco? Because I'm going to have to tell her that there's a reason we called you Frog. Frog legs, for sure. Thin and not much meat."

"No, Suz calls me Cisco. And you're still annoyed that I beat you last month in the Bridesmaids Creek swim."

"I had a leg cramp!" Squint's glare bounced right off Cisco.

"You're a SEAL. You should be in better shape. Anyway, it doesn't matter." He thumped his chest. "You're looking at the new and improved Cisco Grant. And Suz is swimming to win me next weekend."

"Really?" Squint sat up. "Does Daisy know?"

Cisco frowned. "I didn't ask. Guess I didn't care."

"Careful," Squint said. "You misjudge Daisy's fineness. She comes across evil and devilish, but I'm telling you, it's true Texas hot sauce that lady's peddling. And I aim to eat it up, if you'll get out of my way."

"You're going to have to do better than that," Dennis observed. "If you want to win Daisy, Squint, *win* her. Don't get cramps when the race is hot. You must become the rope if you want to lasso her. Frankly, I don't think you have it in you." He shrugged. "Cisco Frog obviously does."

"Cisco Frog!" Cisco glared, worried that pseudonym might stick. "Just Cisco is fine, thanks."

"Well," Sam said, having remained silent this whole time, "I can see that the tie is going to have to go to the runner."

They stared at Sam. Cisco was a bit suspicious. Sam was known for being many things, being clever and underhanded chief among them. In other words, he liked to be in the middle of everything, and turn it inside out just to watch everybody whirl around in different directions thanks to him.

"What runner? We're swimming," Cisco pointed out. "Actually, the girls are swimming."

"Yep." Sam got up and stretched. "And I've entered as a prize."

The men gawked at Sam.

"You can't do that. It's my turn! The ladies want to win *me*. Well, Daisy does. I'm pretty sure Suz is operating out of pity, but I'm not picky," Cisco said.

"Sheesh," Dennis said. "Have some pride, Frog."

Cisco sighed. "Okay. Sam, you can take my place."

The sheriff's office went silent for a moment.

"Did you give up that easily when you were a SEAL?" Dennis demanded. "Just throw in the towel at the first sign of difficulty?"

"No." Cisco looked around the cramped, dark room. A small lamp sat on Dennis's desk. The jail was down the hall, but it was empty now. Dennis's wife, Shirley, had put some potpourri on his desk under the lamp to make it a more "homey" place, she'd said, and it did smell sweet in here. He breathed deeply, trying to clear his head. "You're right. I don't have any pride where Suz is concerned. My brain twirls like a pinwheel when she's around. And she won't kiss me. Says I might be a sloppy kisser."

His best friends thought that was a real thigh-slapper. They roared with laughter. He shrugged, undeterred.

"I've been thinking," Cisco said when the snickers and guffaws died down, "maybe I don't really belong in BC."

They booed that raucously.

"You belong with us," Sam said. "You, me, Squint, we're a team. We were a team in Afghanistan and other places that sometimes felt like hellholes, and sometimes felt real good. But we're a team, and we stick together."

Cisco shook his head now that the words had traveled from his brain to his mouth and hit the atmosphere. "I'm pretty sure the BC rigmarole and fiddle-faddle is beyond me. I'm not cut out for these small-town shenanigans."

"That's right." Squint nodded. "Because you're from a small town in Virginia that grows her boys strapping and proud. No high jinks in those small towns, either."

"It's hard to explain." It wasn't *too* hard to explain— it had to do with what his friends had observed about Suz: she just wasn't into him.

And he was totally into her.

If Daisy won the race, he was a gigged Frog. Two times won and for sure the Bridesmaids Creek charm would kick in. "I don't think Suz is all that motivated to get in shape to win. She was heading off to eat some four-layer cake."

The men didn't laugh like he'd expected.

"Look," Squint said, "Dennis is right. We're going to have to bait your trap better. We'll help you."

"I said nothing like that," Dennis said. "Suz is hometown-grown. She's stubborn and independent, and no one's going to make her do anything she doesn't want to do."

"Which is why," Cisco said after a long, deliberate examination one more time of his options, "I've decided to head back to the rodeo circuit."

"Yeah, right." Sam laughed. "And leave sweet Suz to me?"

"You?" Cisco's gaze jerked to Sam. "Since when has Suz been sweet to you?"

Sam grinned. "I didn't say she had been. I'm saying that you and me setting up a side race—or side bet, whichever you prefer—would make things very interesting."

"Side race?" Cisco was all ears to this.

"Sure. Let's see which one of us can win Suz's heart before the big race. Before you throw in the towel and go get killed by a bull." Sam smiled, glancing around at his brothers before leaning forward to shake Cisco's hand. "May the best man win. Which will be me—and I won't even have to change my name to do it, *Cisco,* my friend."

Chapter Two

Sam was a trickster beyond compare, which was no shock to Cisco. He knew his buddy too well to fall completely for what seemed to be, at first glance, a spirited race between friends. Sam was without doubt trying to encourage him, rally the forces. This was no different than any of the tactics Sam had used in Afghanistan when rallying was needed. He was known for his good humor and slightly wild—okay, zanily wild—approach to life. Stateside, Sam flirted with all the ladies, usually long enough to make certain whatever buddy of his was in the line of fire walked right into said fire.

The problem was, though Cisco wouldn't mention it aloud, Suz *might* have eyes for Handsome Sam, as the brothers-in-arms called him. She certainly didn't seem all that warm to the newly nicknamed Cisco.

Heck, she hadn't even liked his official nom de plume, which he'd been called by his serving brothers.

She'd said he might be a slobbery kisser. And followed that up with *eww*.

There was no point in taking a bet when a man could see that he was on the upside of the teeter-totter. You never knew when your teeter-tottering companion might decide to be funny and hop off, thereby leaving you with a crash landing.

"I don't know. Let's head over to The Wedding Diner and see what's cooking." Cisco got up to his friends' hoots.

"Come on, Cisco," Squint said, "take the bet."

"Yeah, I'm not so sure," Cisco hedged. "Suz said she drew short straw. And I think she's pretty proud of her dog paddle, but hasn't got the stroke part of swimming down yet."

The sheriff wiped tears of laughter from his eyes. "We haven't had so much fun in this town for years. I'm really glad Ty talked you boys into coming to BC." He let out a few more guffaws at Cisco's expense.

"If you're so hot for Daisy," Cisco said to Squint, "do something, I beg you."

"Nope." Squint shrugged. "I like to keep my lasso loose. She'll figure it out eventually, and when she's gotten nice and tired from running after the wrong Prince Charming, she'll be more than happy to let me catch her."

"I've never seen your lasso do anything but droop," Cisco said, sticking the knife in just a little. "I'd like to hear a winning plan."

"You don't exactly sound like you're a cornucopia of options," Squint said.

"Which is why I'm off to eat cake. Nothing bucks a man up and clarifies his thinking like four-layer chocolate cake." Cisco slapped his Stetson down on his head and hurried out of the jail to catch up to Suz, not caring that his buddies seemed to find his prompt exit uproarious.

They just didn't understand the lengths to which he would go to avoid the sexy siren call of Daisy Donovan.

SUZ SAT IN the booth at The Wedding Diner, sipping hot honeyed tea in a delicate flowered china cup, waiting for Cisco to show up, as she hoped he would.

It had been thirty minutes, and he was nowhere to be seen. Quite possibly, the man either couldn't take a hint, or he didn't understand that the proceedings next weekend were quite serious. She was trying to save him from Daisy's clutches, and this was going to require some skill.

First of all, she didn't like frigid water. She didn't fancy swimming in January, though the guys—Squint and Sam, both SEALs—had kitted her out with proper gear so toasty they swore she wouldn't notice the cold.

All she had to do, they claimed, was hop in Bridesmaids Creek and swim like a water moccasin. And Frog—Cisco—would be rescued.

She hadn't wanted to admit that swimming wasn't her forte. Less than her forte. She actually couldn't swim at all.

"You can do it," Jane Chatham, the owner of the diner said. "You can stay afloat, right?"

"I'm pretty proud of my ability to bob like an apple." Suz put her teacup down, glancing at the door. She wondered when Cisco was finally going to come charging in. You'd think the temptation of four-layer cake would have brought him running, but no. The man was a very, very difficult card to play.

"You shouldn't need much to beat Daisy," Cosette Lafleur said. Cosette owned the shop a few doors down, called Madame Matchmaker's Premiere Matchmaking Services. Cosette was BC's resident lucky charm when it came to pairing people up. Only one match so far had backfired on Madame: Suz's sister Mackenzie's first marriage.

Suz was hopeful—determined—that Cosette's wand wouldn't clog up now that Suz actually had a cowboy she wanted in her sights. Cisco, Sam and Squint had drifted to the rodeo circuit after they'd departed the navy, staying together in a tight-knit brotherhood, none of them anxious to return to their own hometowns. Handsome, bad-boy drifters, Ty Spurlock claimed when he brought them to Bridesmaids Creek. Drifters who just needed an anchor—and there were plenty of cute-as-a-button anchors in BC.

Trust Ty to see it that way, drop the load of testosterone on BC and take off for the navy himself after he married spirited redhead Jade Harper.

"I can beat Daisy on any field of battle but water."

"When you were in the Peace Corps all those years," Jane asked, "you didn't have to swim?"

Suz shook her head. "I taught English, I taught math, I helped in the infirmary. I didn't swim. I did, however, assist when there were bites from slithery things." She shivered. "I'm actually not too fond of waterways, if I have to be immersed in them."

"Why didn't you mention this when straws were being drawn?" Cosette demanded. "There were other women who would have gladly gotten the short straw."

"You know very well why." Suz wondered if maybe she should order the cake now. It seemed Cisco wasn't going to show up to join her, which was too bad, because he'd stunned her with that bit about wanting to kiss her. Of course she wasn't going to kiss him!

When he saw her swimming like a demented turtle, he was going to know she wasn't the woman who was destined to be his.

"Why?" Jane demanded, and Suz took a deep breath.

"Both you and Madame Matchmaker know that the Bridesmaids Creek swim has never failed. Neither has the Best Man's Fork run. Except for Mackenzie," she said hurriedly, "and really, I blame that more on my sister's hammerheaded ex than the charms of BC." Or Cosette's matchmaking. Although according to Ty, the whole bad match was his fault.

There were always a few twists and turns in their small town that prided itself on its haunted house, good food and friendly, busybody ways.

"Oh, you're worried about the charm." Cosette nodded wisely, her pink-tinted gray hair shining under the lights of the diner. "You took the straw because you don't want anyone else to have Cisco."

"Maybe it's just a superstition," Suz said. "Maybe we bring this legend on ourselves because we want it so much. When there's a ratio of, what, ten women to every man here? Someone made up a cute gag that claimed that whoever won those swims and races got the man of their dreams at the end. The thing is," Suz said, worried, "we've never had a woman doing the actual competing. It's all wrong. Maybe the legend doesn't work in reverse."

The two women stared at her.

"We don't know," Jane said. "It's never been done."

"Well," Cosette said brightly, "never mind. That's why we have a matchmaker in town."

Suz wished she felt better with Cosette on the case, but there was that teeny matter of the misfire on Mackenzie's first marriage. "Thank you. The thing is, with Daisy determined to win Cisco's heart, I would have done better in a bake-off. Daisy can't cook. And I can't swim."

"Yes, perhaps this didn't get set up properly. But Cisco won Daisy fair and square last month," Cosette reminded them. "He swam the race, he came in first place. The competition was fierce that day, and Squid—"

"Squint," Jane and Suz said, trying to be helpful because on occasion Cosette's native French hit a bump or two.

"Squint had his shot. But he came in dead last." Cosette shook her head. "There'll be no wedding for him in Bridesmaids Creek."

And Squint was the only bachelor who saw Daisy as something she wasn't. The handsome SEAL thought Daisy was a misunderstood bad girl, with a hidden heart of gold.

Although there was as much of a chance that Squint just had the hots for Daisy. Either way, he'd pulled up with a leg cramp, beaten even by Daisy's gang of five bad boys. "Someone needs to save Squint from the legend."

"Could be," Madame Cosette said cheerfully. "But magic isn't really tweakable. What we have here in BC is magic."

"Ty says we're just a town of carneys selling our small-town shtick."

"Is that the word he uses?" Jane wondered.

"When he's being polite. Other times, he goes for a little more flavor in his comments. However, since his marriage to Jade—after the legend worked on his behalf—he's more inclined to lay off the flavoring." Suz breathed a sigh of relief when Cisco appeared in the doorway, backed up by the sheriff, Squint and Sam. She perked up so he'd see her.

It was like he had radar—Suz was sure of it. He came right to their table, doffing his tan Stetson respectfully.

"Ladies," Cisco said.

Cosette squished over next to Jane, both their ample forms filling the booth, so that Cisco would have no choice but to slide in with Suz. Which he did, not appearing to notice their friends' obvious ploy to get them together.

His mind seemed elsewhere, which wasn't good, as far as Suz was concerned.

"What about us?" Sheriff McAdams asked, clearly hoping for an invite to scoot himself and his buddies into the booth, too.

The booth would have accommodated them, but Cosette absently flopped a hand toward an empty one. "That spot's open."

The three men went off, looking comically disappointed. Suz slid a glance at Cisco, checking out his big, handsome, very sexy self.

"Have you had your chocolate cake?" Cisco asked.

She shook her head. Cosette and Jane pushed out of the booth. "I'll get it," Jane said.

"I'll help. Tea or water?" Cosette asked Cisco.

"Milk and coffee, please." He turned to Suz, and Suz's heart seemed to melt inside her.

"Can we talk about the race next weekend?"

She nodded. "Talk away."

"You don't seem all that enthusiastic."

"I'm not." Suz concentrated on the scent of man and

woodsy cologne, and the realization that he seemed to have no intention of taking up the space across the tabletop where Cosette and Jane had left a vacant seat. "I told you, I don't really swim."

He grinned at her, slow and easy, lighting a fire in her body where it hadn't been lit before. "I've taken that into consideration, and I have a plan."

"You do?" Suz stared at his mouth, completely oblivious to Jane plunking down their cake and Cosette spilling a little coffee. You couldn't expect the matchmaker not to be a little nervous, Suz decided when she looked up and realized Cosette was mopping up coffee faster than you could say, "Cleanup in booth one."

She went back to considering Cisco's rugged face.

He smiled at her again, completely ruining her ability to remember that Daisy, the mean, mean girl of Bridesmaids Creek, who'd written the book on mean after her father had scribed the first chapter, had won Cisco just a few short weeks ago. No, all she could think of was why she'd never before realized that Francisco Rodriguez Olivier Grant had such a sexy, steamy set of lips.

She'd been *so* reaching when she'd told him she didn't want to kiss him. Keeping distance was her specialty; she'd done it all her life. The truth was, she was pretty certain and would bet the farm—that being the Hanging H where she and her sister had grown up and currently lived—that this man knew exactly what to do with his mouth in very special, woman-pleasing ways.

He smiled at her. "I'm going to teach you. And when I get done with you, Suz Hawthorne, you're going to be able to swim like a mermaid."

Chapter Three

Holding Suz Hawthorne, even in the cold, cold water of Bridesmaids Creek, was every bit as mind-bending as Cisco had imagined in his dreams, and then some. She was soft and cute and dainty, and there was a part of his body that stayed warm no matter what, just from the contact. He held her plank-style so she could rotate her arms, which she did in paddleboat-wheel fashion.

Staring at her butt in the wet suit wasn't going to make the definitely warm area—a lesser gentleman might even term that area of his body as hard, but thanks to the wet suit it was a concealed difficulty—any less warm. She was like a slippery seal with curves, wriggling in his hands, but she was making a good-faith effort to learn what he was trying to teach. And she hadn't complained about the water temperature once.

Which was the thing he'd always admired about Suz—she was tough. In a delicate sort of way. If she were a man, she would have been a great SEAL candidate.

"You're doing fine. But that's enough for today." Cisco helped Suz from the water to the bank, ostensibly guiding her so she wouldn't slip and fall back in, but really so he could keep his hands on her a little longer under the respectable guise of swim coach.

"So what do you think?" Suz faced him as she toweled off. It looked like she might want to shiver a little, but wasn't going to give in to it.

Secretly, he was dismayed by the fact that Suz really couldn't swim. "At this short-straw party that was held in my honor, did you happen to mention to anyone that you couldn't swim very well?"

Suz shook out her hair. "No. I didn't think I'd be short straw. I've always been pretty lucky."

So she didn't think swimming for him was necessarily a good thing. Cisco was about to move on to his next salient question, namely: Was there anything else she could think of to be done to avoid the Curse, as he now thought of Bridesmaids Creek's very potent charms, when the nightmare of his nightmares roared up on her shiny motorcycle.

Daisy hopped off, shed her helmet and glared. "What's going on?"

"Cisco's giving me a swimming lesson." Suz fluffed her hair, spraying a few final water droplets. "What's going on with you?"

Daisy's glare could have cut fog. "You're *cheating*."

This didn't sound good. Cisco decided he'd best intervene, but before he could say anything, Daisy got back on her bike. "I'm filing a formal complaint with the Bridesmaids Creek committee. You know very well that you're not supposed to be doing anything to influence the prize, Suz Hawthorne."

Suz stiffened up like a fierce chicken. "How am I influencing the prize? Cisco's giving me a lesson. There's nothing else going on."

Daisy's gaze slid to him. "You're not being impartial."

"Guilty as charged." There was no point in denying it. "Look, Daisy, I know there's this enchantment, or airy-fairy nonsense, that appears to be pretty baked here in this town, but I don't care how many curses you put on me, I'm just not going to be into you." He swallowed, hating to hurt her feelings but realizing that bluntness was needed before the threat of committees got thrown around some more. He didn't know what strength a BC committee had, but there was already enough bad blood in the town as it was. "I don't care how many times you win me, I'm not the guy for you. I'm sorry."

Daisy shook her head. "That's the beauty of the charms here. Sometimes we don't know what's right under our noses."

He looked over Suz's seal-slick figure, eyeing her curves and her streaked hair. "I know what's under my nose. I don't need any race or contest or matchmaker to tell me."

Daisy frowned. "I'm going to file a complaint. Once again, the Hawthornes have conspired to work things to their advantage. Suz, you've tampered with the race, and that's just not done in BC. Our legends are sacrosanct."

Suz shrugged. "File away. I don't care. It was just a swimming lesson."

"Just because you've always been the hometown princess doesn't mean you can break the rules." Daisy zoomed off.

"Hell, I'm sorry. I didn't realize we were bending any contest rules." Cisco shook his head. "I don't want to be the damn prize. I only swam the first race because her dad was putting up a huge purse, and my buddies and I decided to win it and give it to charity. And we looked forward to putting a major thumping on Daisy's gang." He shook his head. "Didn't foresee Squint, of all people, cramping up and crab-crawling into last place."

Suz walked to his truck. "So don't be the prize, if it bugs you so much. It's just a moneymaker for our town. People like to come out and see the event, the same folks who frequent our haunted house at the Hanging H. Families who like family events they can go to with their kids."

"It's a big deal, huh?" A little guilt seeped into him.

She shrugged and got into his truck. "I told you, it's a fund-raiser, a community-building event, and we enjoy tooting our own horn here. With Robert Donovan trying to tear this town down, we encourage family-friendly events, hoping to tempt people to settle here."

He started the truck, noting that the guilt was rising inside him. "But it's so silly."

She smiled, brushed her wet hair straight back from her forehead in a slick tail. He had an even better look at her face sans jewelry and hair, and realized Suz wasn't just pretty, she had a fine-boned beauty to her that was stunning. "It seems silly to you. You're not from here. I might think things in your town are silly, too. Or at least unusual."

"Yeah. Probably." He drove down the road toward the Hanging H to drop her back home. Then he'd trudge over to the bunkhouse, where his buddies would be waiting to rib him. "What would happen if I fell for someone else?" he asked, his voice deliberately casual, his heart banging like mad. "Even though Daisy won me—which is kind of a bogus win, because I was really swimming lights-out to win her dad's dough to donate to charity, and to beat her gang, which was awesome—" he took a deep breath "—but I wasn't trying to win *her*."

"So you're saying that the legend might not work because you had ulterior motives?" Suz looked at him.

"I'm just asking." He went back to his original question. "So, theoretically speaking, what would happen if I fell for, say, you? Wouldn't that negate the charm?"

"It's never happened. We've always operated within the bounds of what's worked all these years. Never tried to circumvent the system." She studied him. "You really don't like Daisy, do you?"

"No," he said, pretty desperately. "I'm not a superstitious guy, but you folks are giving me the heebie-jeebies with all this charm stuff. I don't believe it, but there may be something in the water, because I never dreamed I'd see Ty Spurlock settle down. Ever."

"Yeah, that was a shocker." Suz shrugged, put on some shiny, clear lip gloss. "So don't be part of the swim."

"It's that easy?"

She turned to him, surprised. "Of course! No one's forcing you to participate in our town functions."

Town dysfunctions. He wondered if he was being a dud over what was arguably probably just a fun day in January, something to break up the monotony of an otherwise cold, dreary month.

How he wished Suz was the prize. For *her*, he was pretty certain he could set new swimming records. "I know you can beat her. I'm not worried."

Suz's delicate heart-shaped lips separated. "You're not?"

Cisco took a deep breath. "Nope."

"Because you sounded like you were a second ago."

"I feel pretty good with my champion," he said, smiling at Suz. "And we've got a few more days to teach you. You've got this."

Suz smiled. "Thanks."

"No problem." He pulled into the Hanging H's long drive. "It's going to be fun. And I saw on the weather report it's going to be an unseasonably warm day Saturday. Everything's in your corner."

She brightened. "Thanks for believing in me."

"Never doubted you."

He got out of the truck, and she hopped out, too. She waved goodbye, and went into her house. Cisco took a deep, fortifying breath, and slunk into the bunkhouse to face the teasing he knew he would receive.

Squint and Sam lounged on the leather sofas, drinking what looked like hot cocoa and eating bonbons, Cisco thought with disgust. "Are those chocolate drops you fellows are dropping into your maws?"

"Mmm." Squint grinned. "They're called cake balls, but they're really more chocolate or vanilla frosting than a piece of cake. Here." Squint tossed him one, which Cisco caught, popping it into his mouth after studying it.

It was sweet, but he'd rather go to Suz for his sugar intake. "Don't you fellows have anything to do? Besides sit around in the lap of luxury?"

"Actually, we're waiting on you for the swim report." Sam grinned. "We've already heard from Daisy."

"Great." Cisco pondered the beer in the fridge, decided to hit the whiskey instead.

"Self-medicating?" Sam asked, and his buddies guffawed.

"Do I need to?" Cisco came out with three glasses

and a full bottle. "Anybody joining me this cold evening?"

"Sure. We'll toast your doom," Sam said.

"Hey! That's my girl you're talking about," Squint said. "Daisy is not *doom*. She's a radioactively hot baby." He smacked his lips after taking a shot. "I wish I was the prize so she could win me."

"Take my place." Cisco shrugged. "Everybody wins."

"Oh, ye of little faith." Sam looked pleased. "Don't you think Suz can steal Daisy's crown? Daisy was in here, madder than a hornet. She seems to think you're giving Suz tips—SEAL tips—on how to win."

"Suz can't steal Daisy's crown yet." Cisco raised his glass to his buddies, took another shot. "But I have faith."

His friends grinned at him. "You're being dishonest," Sam said. "Your eyelid always jumps when you're deviating from the truth."

"Otherwise known as lying like a rug." Squint held out his glass for a refill. "It's okay. We get it. But just know my girl was awfully PO'd. She's going to make some noise about your gaming the holy BC system. And I don't know what happens then."

"All hell breaks loose. Who cares?" Cisco shrugged. "There were no tips given. Since Suz can't swim, it's not like I can give her a SEAL tip, although I appreciate Daisy's faith in our navy."

Sam and Squint looked startled. "Can't swim?" Squint repeated, sounding dumbfounded.

"Not a stroke." Cisco eyed his glass, appreciating the amber liquid. It was smooth, as smooth as the slick wet suit that looked as if it had been spray-painted on Suz, much to his appreciative gaze. "It's okay. She's got the race in the bag. I'll be saved, and then you can press your case on the unsuspecting Daisy." He stared down Squint. "If Daisy's 'your girl,' as you call her, why hasn't she figured that out?"

Squint shrugged. "It seems her gaze is caught on your ugly mug."

Cisco laughed. "You *are* a rather homely dog."

"Thank you." Squint leaned back in the sofa. "You want me to help you teach Suz how to swim? I really need her to win this race, for the obvious reason."

"You?" Sam laughed along with Cisco. "Leg Cramp Man? Mr. Last Place?"

Squint looked devastated. "Never happened before."

"You'll redeem yourself one day." A bright, shiny idea illuminated Cisco's brain. "Have you told Daisy how you feel?"

"No, dude, that's not smooth." Squint didn't look optimistic.

"It's because he came in last place in the swim last month," Sam said, filling in the missing pieces Squint didn't want to admit. "We overheard Daisy telling someone that she would never date a man who came in last place, behind her gang. That man, of course, was our buddy."

Squint's face mapped misery like a human Etch A Sketch. "It was a muscle spasm! People get them!"

Cisco looked at the ceiling, wondering how to salvage the dilemma they found themselves in. "We'll figure it out. All for one, and one for all, the way it's always been." He looked at his friend speculatively. "You believe in all this hocus-pocus around here?"

"Ty swears by it. He's the one who would know," Squint said. "He's born and bred BC."

"You?" Cisco asked Sam.

"Hell, I don't care." Sam grinned. "I'm always going to do whatever I want, and no charm's going to change that."

"The selfish bachelor." Cisco nodded. "But not as selfish as you," he said, looking at Squint. "If you have such a hot thing going for Daisy, why don't you just tell her? It could change everything for all of us. Take me out of the boiling pot."

"But frogs belong in boiling pots," said Squint, clearly unbothered by his best friend's dilemma. "I can't tip my hand. I'll just wait, as I've said, until she's done chasing after what she doesn't want. Women do that, you know. It's all part of the dance." He relaxed into the sofa cushions, a look of contentment on his face. "I do wish you wouldn't get my girl all stirred up, though. Makes me sad to see her unhappy."

Cisco scoffed. "Let's get on with the planning of this escapade. It's time for teamwork."

"What escapade?" Sam asked.

"Like last time, when we all swam the race together to achieve a unified goal. Teamwork. That's what we're good at."

His good buddies looked blank as new sheets of paper.

"No plan here," Sam said. "I've even changed my mind about participating in the race. No reason to since Daisy's going to win. So, just call me No Plan Sam."

"I've got nothing," Squint agreed.

Suz blew in on a gust of cold air, warming Cisco. She looked fresh and invigorated from their lesson: hair dry and spiky, foxy smile on her face, roses in her cheeks to match the pink scarf around her neck. He was definitely warm for this woman, in all the right places.

"I brought pumpkin chocolate chip muffins," Suz said, and the men cheered.

"Just the thing to go with whiskey." Ever the dog, Sam hopped up to help himself first to what Cisco considered his spoils.

"My work, my prize," Cisco said, snatching the cute basket with the blue-and-white patterned napkin away from Sam. "Sit down and stay a second," he said to Suz, guiding her to a seat far away from Sam and Squint.

"Yes, do." Sam gazed at Suz, waiting his turn at the basket, which Cisco now passed around grudgingly. "We've been hearing about your lesson this morning."

Suz glanced with some annoyance at Cisco, which he felt was ill-deserved. "That should be a private topic."

"Yeah, well," Squint said, pawing the basket with his big hand. "Daisy came by to throw a hissy about Cisco cheating. She's filing a complaint, or squawking to someone."

Suz frowned. "Let her complain. We did nothing wrong."

Cisco perked at the sound of "we" on Suz's sweet lips, very much liking the "we're in this together" medley. "Besides which, I have a plan to completely neutralize our town tattletale."

"Watch it," Squint reminded him, "again, that's my girl we're talking about."

"Precisely. And I have a thunderbolt of inspiration about your girl," Cisco said. "Squint, Mr. Leg Cramp Extraordinaire, is going to take my place on Saturday."

The room went dead silent as everyone stared at him.

"To what end?" Squint demanded.

"If Daisy needs to win someone, then it should be you. That will undo the curse—"

"Charm!" everyone reminded him.

"And Squint will then be the object of this match-maker-created charm."

"How do you know that's how we got the charm?" Suz asked. "It's top secret. Only a few people know."

Cisco looked at Suz. "What's top secret?"

"Never mind," Suz said. "Continue with your idea."

"His explosion of brain cells is top secret," Sam said.

"His deviation from the norm," Squint said. "I don't like how you're trying to cheat my lady out of her win." He wagged a finger at Cisco. "I know when you're trying to think up an outside-the-box strategy, watched you do it many times in Afghanistan. And this feels like that."

"It always worked, didn't it?" His friends nodded. Cisco took great pride in his ability to strategize when things look bleak—and right now, they were bleak. "Daisy will win Squint, because he, not I, will be at the finish line. The charm will ricochet on to Squint, and he will get the woman of his dreams, and I'll be free. Happy ending for all," he said cheerily, settling back with a pumpkin chocolate chip muffin clutched in one hand and his whiskey in the other. "Let the applause begin."

Suz hopped to her feet, not applauding. "You don't think I can win."

Cisco hesitated. "Now, I didn't say that—"

"Yeah, you did," Sam said. "Pretty much you did."

"It's implied," Squint said, "and it's a bit sad, if you ask me."

He wasn't about to bring up Suz's lack of swimming

prowess, but wasn't it obvious he was trying to save her from embarrassment? And holy hell, he didn't want anywhere near this top-secret whatchamagig charm thing, just in case it did work. He was *not* winding up at an altar with Daisy Donovan, thus losing the woman of his dreams, and taking Squint's, which would mean losing a good buddy.

This called for clear digestion of cold, hard facts. "Suz, beautiful, you really don't swim. It's more of a dog paddle that goes sort of circular. It keeps you from drowning, but that's its main utilitarian function."

His buddies drew in sharp breaths, gave him the *no-no-no* slashing signs to signal him to silence himself before it was too late.

It was too late.

Suz went to the door. "Fine. We'll do it your way. Squint, be at the finish line. Be sure you have a warm blanket waiting for me, and get your pucker ready."

She went out as cold gushed in the door, slamming it behind her.

"Smooth," Sam observed.

"Oh, boy," Squint said, "you've stepped in a big ol' pile of steamy·trouble you are never getting off your boot."

Cisco ate his muffin in silence, dreading Saturday even more, now that his sweet 'n' petite dollface had mentioned puckering to Squint. She'd talked about a pucker once to him, saying kissing him would force her to pucker like she'd bit into a grapefruit.

But she hadn't said that to Squint. In fact, she'd sounded like the pucker she had waiting for him was going to be served up with a smile.

Chapter Four

In the end, Suz won the race handily, due to Daisy coming up with a leg cramp in the last fifty yards—a Squint-styled leg cramp, Cisco presumed, realizing now that the fix had been in, thanks to his dumb bright idea. With a couple hundred people posted along the banks of Bridesmaids Creek with hot cocoa, pompons and enthusiastic yells for both wet-suit-wearing women, Daisy must have calculated enough effort to put in a great show, then pulled up—because she didn't want Squint.

She wanted Cisco.

Surprised by how many folks turned out for this event—both in-towners and out-of-towners, Cisco realized BC had their charmed ways, which made them money and made them special. It didn't matter whether the charms were real or not, but what did matter was Suz giving Squint the kiss Cisco wanted.

Realizing he was now double-cursed—double-charmed, call it how you saw it—Cisco knew he had one option left to him. So he packed up his stuff, turned his notice in to Justin Morant, Suz's sister Mackenzie's husband, tossed his duffel into his truck and headed to the rodeo circuit.

Just plain ol' Frog now. "I apparently am the frog

that got put back in the pond," he said, turning on some country-western tunes to commiserate with him as he sang his way into New Mexico. He'd start off in Santa Fe, work his way into shape.

Thought about Suz's swimming skills a lot on the way, and how happy she'd looked rising out of the water, victorious. The blue-haired sylph had put a lot of effort into refining her stroke over the week, and a little shame crept into him that he'd doubted her.

That was not hero material. No wonder she'd not even glanced his way at the finish line.

So tonight was his first ride. Frog got his number pinned on, went to shoot the breeze with the fellows. It wasn't going to be easy to establish the kind of friendships he had with his team back in BC. But when you were a renegade persona non grata, you bucked up and moved along.

"How you doing, buddy?" Someone clapped him on the back, but Frog didn't see who it was as they went by. He waited for his name to be called, rode a respectable ride, but without a decent enough number to make it into the next round he pushed on to the next rodeo.

Two weeks later, the blue-haired angel of his dreams appeared beside the chute in Arizona where his bull was about to be loaded. "Suz!"

She nodded. "Yes. You big chicken-hearted weasel."

"I suppose I deserve that."

"You *do* deserve that." She glared at him. "After you ride, I want to talk to you, buster."

Gladly was what he wanted to say. His eyes ate her up. "Okay. I'll be out in eight," he said, posturing a little.

She scoffed and went to the grandstand. He grinned. "Things are looking up, ol' buddy," he told the bull being loaded. "Look out for me. My name is all over you."

The bull thought little of his comments, and tossed him in under two seconds—well, maybe two seconds, but the guys later said it was doubtful—and stomped him a little just to make his point. Frog writhed in the gritty arena, helped out quick by a couple of bullfighters.

Suz met him, her eyes huge. "Are you all right?"

"Except for a missing gizzard or two, I should be fine. Maybe my stomach muscles are papier-mâché, but they should strengthen back up eventually. A year from now," he said, falling with a groan into the chair the bullfighters steered him to. A rodeo doctor ran over, checking him out, proclaiming he just needed rest and TLC and maybe some kisses for his ouchies.

Nobody laughed. Even Frog knew it had been a near thing.

"Come on, you big baby." Suz helped him to his feet. "Where's your room?"

"I sleep in my truck," he said, feeling pain radiate from the roof of his mouth to the soles of his feet.

"Well, we're getting a room."

"I like the sound of that," he said, meaning he could use a lengthy lie-down in a real bed to try to get his innards back to 3-D shape and regular form rather than smashed flat as peanut butter.

"Settle down, cowboy. I'm going to nurse you back to health, and that's it."

"Thank you," he managed to gasp out as she folded him into a human accordion into his own truck and drove to find a hotel. "What are you doing here?"

"I told you. I came to bless you out for being such

a faithless knucklehead. I'm not surprised at all to see you in this shape. You're clearly a man who doesn't learn easily."

"This may be true." He caught a whiff of perfume and something else sweet, like sexy woman, something he hadn't smelled in his truck in a long time. "That's the only reason you're here? You could have blessed me out by cell phone."

"Not near as satisfying as in person." She stopped outside a cozy B and B and looked at him. "Looks like doilies for drapes. Can you handle this much toile and chintz?"

"All I do is toil and whatever else you said." He felt like he was time traveling out of his head a bit. "Good luck finding a room."

"Be right back."

He sighed when she left because the intoxicating scent went with her. God, he was glad to see her. Shocked as all get-out, but glad.

And that's when it hit him like a bundle of thunderbolts sent from above: he had a thing for Suz Hawthorne. And not just any old thing—he was head over heels for her. Irretrievably and irrevocably. From the stiffy in his jeans to the grin on his face when she was around, he was in love with that little fireball.

She tore open his door, jumping him clean out of his stupefied reverie. "She has one room. For the record, we're married."

"Hot damn." She helped him out of the truck, a slow, painful effort on his behalf. "I knew you'd get me one way or another. That swim must have worked, after all."

"Just keep walking to bungalow number three, and

if you could turn the motor off your mouth, it would be ever so nice."

"That BC shtick knew you were meant to be mine," he said, groaning torturously when she helped him to the bed. He climbed in ungracefully. "I'm sorry, but I'm not going to be able to provide you with any marital bliss at the moment."

She laughed, and it kind of flattened his ego again.

"I'm going out to get us some food. Lie there and don't do anything else stupid."

Suz flashed out the door. Frog tossed his hat away. "Stupid?" he asked. "Anything *else* stupid?"

What had she meant by that? He couldn't remember doing anything stupid. She hadn't put the remote by him, and he was too sore to reach the cell phone in his back pocket, so he lay there like a suffering succotash until he awakened, realizing she was back in his room, and he smelled the delicious fragrance of home-cooked food.

"You shouldn't have, beautiful," he said.

"Shouldn't have what?"

"Cooked for me." He sniffed the air again without opening his eyes. "Smells like the Hanging H in here. I've missed that place."

"That's nice. Try to get some of this soup down your fast-talking gullet."

Well, that didn't sound very nice. Frog started to question her comment, realized the soup was quite tasty. "Why are you really here?"

"I told you. I want a baby."

Alarm bells sounded in his head. He sat up, pushed the soup away. "Wait. I don't remember any conversation about a baby."

She laughed. "Just seeing how out of it you really are."

"I'm not *that* out of it." In fact, not only was he in pain right now, he was good and rattled. "Wait a minute, you're not here on a baby-making mission, are you? Because that's what Jade did to Ty, you know, and before he knew it, he was…"

She looked at him and his words trailed off. "He was what?"

"Well, married. First he was a father, of course, which he was the last one to know about, and then he was married." Now that he thought about it, that string of events actually had a nice ring to it. "Hey! I didn't like you kissing Squint! It looked a little enthusiastic to me, especially for a girl who'd just swum a race and should have been lacking oxygen."

She gave him a look he would distinctly term as disbelieving. "Don't be an ape. I don't ask who you kiss."

"I haven't kissed anyone! Not since Ty dragged us all to BC for brides." He frowned. "Now that I think about that, that's unnatural. Kiss me."

"I don't think so. Eat."

"You kissed Squint." He didn't want to eat. What he wanted was Suz's mouth, and she didn't seem too inclined to share those sexy lips of hers. "That doesn't seem right. You would have kissed me, if I'd been at the finish line." He experienced some serious regret that he'd had such little faith in his blue-streaked bombshell. "And you didn't seem too pained about kissing him, either."

"It was like kissing a big old gummy bear. Soft, and kind of sweet." She dug a brownie out of the bag for him. "You weren't at the finish line, so you forfeited."

This didn't sound promising. "So why are you really here?" Maybe she'd pursue the baby angle again. That at least sounded like it might culminate in some kissing.

"Because the committee has decided that a third race is going to have to be run."

"What?" Frog put down his brownie. "Why?"

"Because you cheated the magic, and Daisy's raising the roof. Says you didn't operate under good faith and then ran off like a scared dog." Suz looked at him and shook her head. "As much as I like to disagree with Daisy about anything and everything, she has a right to her grievance."

"I don't get it." What was the deal with this town and their competitive streak?

"Daisy did win you fair and square the first time. I challenged for you, but you cheated the magic, so the committee has decided that the tie must be broken."

"How?" He was agog by the fact that Suz would have come this far to tell him all this, which let him know the situation was serious. "What if I don't want to come back?" This was going to start the whole you-didn't-believe-I-could-win thing with Suz, too, and that was trouble he didn't want between them right now. After all, he was in a comfy bed, and she was sitting on it, and romance could happen if a man was patient, right?

"If you don't come back, I'm afraid Squint will never get Daisy."

"Daisy doesn't want Squint. He's not the catch he thinks he is," Frog groused. "I appear to be said catch."

"And we can't figure out why." Suz shook her head, shooting his confidence chock-full of holes. "You certainly haven't proven yourself on the field of battle."

His jaw dropped. "I most certainly did!"

"BC's field of battle," she said. "Our battles are different."

"I'll say." He was entirely disgruntled now. "Jeez, a guy makes a little mistake, and he pays. Let the wrong woman decide he's sex candy, and he's toast."

"Cisco," Suz said, and he perked up, realizing that he was Cisco again and not the hapless Frog, "it really hurt my feelings that you didn't believe I'd win the race."

There was the crux of the matter. He'd been a real heel, and he knew it. "I'm sorry about that, Suz. I really am. I was trying to make life easier for everyone."

"We're not about easy in BC. We're about the magic."

"I just don't believe much in airy-fairy stuff."

"It's because you don't let yourself feel it."

"I don't know. I got dragged to those *Twilight* movies. I'm telling you, I laughed at all that supposed angst. I think I'm a straight-line kind of guy, no deviating."

"It's probably a SEAL thing," Suz said.

"No, Squint's superstitious as hell. And Sam, whoa. He won't even pet a black cat." He bit into the brownie, which was very good, but not as good as Suz's mouth would be, he was quite certain. "I wore a saint medal in Afghanistan that Squint gave me. Saint Michael." He pulled it out of his shirt to show her. "I think it saved my life."

She smiled. "Why don't you get some rest?"

He glanced around the blue-and-white room. Suz was right: there were a few delicate doilies in the smallish room, but it was a comfortable place. The bed comforter was soft and puffy, the sheets clean and soft. The bed itself was large, but not too large that he couldn't envision himself eventually wrapping himself around Suz's cute, sexy little bod. There was an en suite bath, and two lamps with stained glass on either side of the bed. "I'm glad you're here," he said, more gruffly than he intended.

"I'm glad I'm here, too." She got up, pulled a blanket from the large closet and an extra pillow from the shelf, tossed them onto the floor. "Get some rest. You're going to feel the pain by morning."

He set the brownie down, put the sack of food on the nightstand. "What are you doing?"

"I've been driving all day to find you. I'm going to sleep. Good night." She snuggled down into her pallet, which did look quite comfy, but which wasn't his bed.

"Get in bed. I promise I won't touch you." He wouldn't like keeping that promise, but he couldn't bear the thought of her sleeping on the floor.

"I'm fine. I was in the Peace Corps. This is heaven compared to some of the places I've slept. Will you turn off the lamp when you're ready?"

Cisco leaned back against the pillow. This was not good. She belonged up here with him, in his arms.

But as she'd so gently pointed out, he hadn't proved himself on the field of BC battle. In fact, it sounded like the town thought he had some ground to make up, some refurbishing of his reputation.

Which he had a feeling meant he was getting none of Suz until he performed said miracle. "Hey, Suz," he said, leaning back over the bed to stare down at her.

She was tucked nicely into her nest of covers. She looked up at him. "Yes?"

"What kind of race are they wanting to run this time? And when is it?"

"It's in a week. Next Saturday."

He hesitated. There was a plum-size goiter on his

ankle from where he'd gotten a little extra stomp from the bull, not to mention his general soreness and the fact that he felt like a gingerbread man, pretty one-dimensional. "You want me to swim in a week?"

Suz yawned, a delicate yawn that had him arrested by the sight of perfect teeth and a pink tongue, and a mouth he wished would kiss him. "Actually, the committee thinks the tie will go to the runner."

"You mean it's a Best Man's Fork run?" This was even worse. In water, where he had the most skills and would at least be buoyant, maybe his body would hold up.

"Yes." She smiled at him. "You should rest up. You're going to need the restorative powers of sleep."

He stared down into those gorgeous eyes, sunk in desire for her. "I'm going to be running with one leg tied behind my back, so to speak."

"Now you know how I felt. I expect you'll rise to the occasion. Good night, Cisco." Suz rolled over, nestling down, and Cisco turned off the lamp.

He was beginning to wonder if all of Bridesmaids Creek was conspiring against him ever getting the girl. There was certainly nothing magical about their particular brand of matchmaking where he was concerned.

And he wasn't quite sure how to turn the tide his way.

Chapter Five

Suz got up in the night to check on Cisco. He really hadn't looked all that well after the bull had done its fancy footwork on him. She'd tried to be breezy and cool about the whole thing, but her heart had been firmly lodged in her throat. As a matter of fact, she didn't want to ever see him on a bull again.

She slipped into the shower, being careful not to awaken him, though she wasn't sure it was possible to disturb him unless she set off a cherry bomb in the room. The man slept like a log, comfortably wedged against the pillow, sitting up, one arm behind his head. It was the first time she'd really seen him asleep, without a shirt on, wearing only tight black briefs, revealed by the gentle glow of the bathroom light when she opened the door.

The door now closed behind her, Suz shut her eyes for just a minute. Whoa, how had she missed those lanky limbs and that muscled abdomen? Cisco was a good-looking man, but naked he was something to behold. Sexy, white-hot, worthy of very pleasant dreams.

No wonder Daisy had set her cap so tightly for him.

"Suz?"

She cracked the door open. "Yes?"

"Oh. I thought you were still on the floor. You okay?"

"I'm fine. Just taking a shower. I didn't mean to wake you."

"You didn't. I was craving one of those brownies you brought and didn't want to rustle the bag if you were asleep." He grabbed it, pulling out the last brownie. "Want a bite?"

A bite of you, yes. Suz shook her head. "No. But thanks."

Suz closed the door, showered, sighing as the warm water washed over her. Thought about Cisco lying out there a bit beat up, wondered how he was going to be up to speed for next weekend. She dried her short hair with a towel, pulled on some pajama shorts and a top from her duffel and walked out to find Cisco munching happily on his brownie and calling for pizza.

"Really? At this hour?" Suz asked. "It's 2:00 a.m."

"Would you rather have something else? The only other thing I can get delivered in this town at this hour is doughnuts."

"I can wait four hours until a coffee shop opens for breakfast." She plopped down on the bed next to him, flipped on the TV.

"Uh, you know what? Cancel that order, please," Cisco said, hanging up. "A western omelet sounds really good before I ride."

Suz stiffened. "You're not planning to do that, are you?"

"I am. I have to, or I don't make it into the next round."

She stared at him. "The doctor won't clear it. Besides which, weren't you disqualified? You have to have been. The bull won."

"Oh, ye of little faith. I have another ride coming to

me. I have to ride or I lose my chance at points. Which is bad for my next rodeo."

"Cisco, you don't get it." He really didn't understand that she couldn't witness him suffering bodily harm again. "You have to rest for next weekend."

"Aw, kitten." He touched her cheek. "Don't you worry about me. I promise you I suffered much worse when I was in the navy."

"That was then and this is now." Suz tried to think how she could convince him that he totally wanted no more part of rodeo. "Come back to BC, Cisco. The rodeo circuit isn't for you. I mean, look at you."

Yes, indeed, look at him, all six-foot-two worth of god-bodied hunkiness. It was all she could do to tear her eyes away and think rationally. Not think about slipping those tight black boxers off him and—

No, no, no. "Cisco, look. There are just some things in life one has to accept. I'm not a good swimmer, and you're not a good bull rider."

He grinned. "Don't sell me short, beautiful. I was doing well until a certain sexy doll blew my focus today. And I'm determined to get better."

"And lose all your major organs in the process." She shook her head. "I vote you give up rodeo. Come back to BC."

"Nope. I belong here." He ruffled her hair affectionately. "You cute little Smurf-haired thing. I like it when you act all concerned."

"I'm not concerned." Suz glared at him. "I'm just protecting the race."

"So? It's not like I'm ever going to be free of Daisy. Why do you think I'm here?" He shook his head. "I'm never going back. I don't believe in all that silly juju, but Daisy's convinced that I'm the man of her starry slumbers. And since my buddy has his tail in a knot over her, BC's a bad place for me to be. It's the fastest way I know of to lose a friend. And I worked real hard not to lose his gnarly ass in Afghanistan. Not gonna lose our friendship over a spoiled daddy's girl."

Suz took a deep breath. "That's the other thing. Daisy went kind of gonzo when you left. She's pretty sure you and I cooked up some kind of plan together to cheat her of her one chance at the charm."

He looked at her. "I don't understand."

"Daisy thinks you and I have a secret thing going on."

"That would be interesting indeed. But not true."

Suz pulled the covers up to her neck and sank against the pillow, her gaze melting into his and desperately trying to avoid staring at the sexy muscled abs leading right down to a no doubt very desirable area of his body. "Daisy had her father start foreclosure proceedings on the new addition being built at the Hanging H. Which means there won't be any expansion to the haunted house this year."

"Why?"

"She's like her dad. Determined to have her way." Suz shrugged. "Since I live at the Hanging H with Mackenzie and Justin and the babies, and since the Haunted H is our family business—" she took a deep breath "—and since she thinks you and I scuttled her big day at Bridesmaids Creek…"

"And that we have a secret thing," he added.

"Yes. She's taking it out on our home and business. Besides that, she's also talked her father into finally squeezing Cosette and Phillipe out of their businesses.

Robert owns the company that has their financing. There'll be no more Madame Matchmaker and Monsieur Unmatchmaker located in the center of BC, where they belong. Where they've been for years."

The whole situation was devastating. She had to make Cisco see how badly they needed him to take on this challenge.

"Hmm." He pondered that, rubbing his chest absently, which Suz really wished didn't have her quite so mesmerized. "Has anyone tried talking to her?"

"I have. She won't listen. She caught us that day."

"The swimming lesson."

She didn't reply. He picked up her hand, held it in his bigger one, which felt comforting.

"Who taught you to swim so well by Saturday? I noticed a definite improvement in your skills. And Daisy was stunned."

"Sam."

"I knew it!" Cisco laughed, and it was a pleasant, rich sound that had her nerves practically jumping with its sexy appeal. Not to mention how nice it would be to put her head on that big, strong chest, let her hand roam down that trail—

"There's only one way to solve this."

She looked at him. "How?"

He rolled onto his side, pulled her face close to his. "We need to start a secret thing. Right now."

"What would that solve?"

"I don't know. But if I'm accused, I'd like to be guilty. I've never had a secret thing. It sounds fun." He kissed her fingertips. "The only thing is, I'm not entirely sure you've told me everything."

Suz cleared her throat a trifle nervously. "Like what?"

"Like the real reason you want me in BC."

She squirmed a bit, Cisco's rock-hard body giving her own body fits she had to ignore. "I told you. The committee has decided the fair thing to do is to hold a tiebreaker."

"But the magic is the magic. It doesn't care about ties, if I understand magic. The first race is the one that would matter, since you didn't win me the second race, either."

She lowered her gaze from his piercing perusal of her. "We've never tested BC's magic before. We just don't know."

"What would change Daisy thinking she wants me?"

"Maybe if you go out with her, show her what you're really like."

"Not gonna happen."

"I just know Squint could beat you if you guys ran the Best Man's Fork," Suz said a bit desperately. "And now that you're all banged up, he'd really have a shot!"

"Oh, I see." He laughed. "You want me to throw the race, so Daisy will see Mr. Leg Cramp as the big guy. The more desirable specimen."

"In a word, yes."

"And then, if she has her own man, by her own choice, she might give up on foreclosing." He lingered over her fingertips, nibbling, sending shivers up and down Suz's back. "That's the game, my little Smurf, and the real reason you want me to go back with you. You've been sent to find me, meaning you drew short straw once again. You're to bring me back, have me race and lose to my buddy so he can be the conquering hero.

Thus will Daisy have a new love, and in her newfound state of happiness she will cease the legal proceedings that have the town in a twist. Because as we all know, as goes the Hanging H, so go the fortunes of Bridesmaids Creek." He gave her a steady look, a half smile on his lips. "What you're asking me to do, Suz Hawthorne, is to save Bridesmaids Creek."

She sniffed. "Okay."

He smiled. "I lived in BC long enough to know how the crafty minds works there. All this talk about you wanting to have a baby, and you acting all worried about me—that's all a smoke screen."

"Not entirely," Suz said defensively. "I am worried about you. I've seen children tear up toys more gently than that bull lit into you."

He leaned back against his pillow. "I don't believe a word of your story. You want me to return to throw a race to my buddy." He shook his head. "And if Squint gets another so-called leg cramp, am I supposed to walk to let him beat me?"

"In your present condition," Suz began, and Cisco pulled her to him, effectively silencing her by kissing her, invading her mouth, stealing her senses. Suz realized she was in trouble; this wasn't like kissing the big ol' gummy bear, as she'd called Squint. No, this was all rock-hard, demanding man, slightly annoyed man, who had ideas of his own about how he wanted things to go.

His mouth wasn't soft on hers, and she didn't want to be anywhere but in Cisco's arms. In fact, of all the guessing Cisco had done about why she was really here, why she'd actually sought him out, he'd hit a lot of the reasons why she'd been sent to find him—and not hit on the one reason why she'd actually come.

She *wanted* him.

She got as close to him as she could, and he tucked his hand under her fanny, pulling her closer still. Suz practically melted from the hot nearness and the rising heat taking her over.

When he released her, Suz gasped with surprise. And a fervent wish that he hadn't.

"Now, little lady," Cisco said, "you've had your say. I've listened to all the malarkey and whatsis from the BC crowd that I intend to. Here's the deal. I don't care what anyone prognosticates or sees in their crystal ball. The sky could open up and Zeus could hit me with a thunderbolt, and I still wouldn't be damaged enough to go for Daisy Donovan. It should be perfectly clear to you by now that I want a thing with you, and I don't care if it's secret or not. I'm sorry your place is getting foreclosed on, but I'm not your magic carpet ride to salvation for that, either. In other words, I'm not the hero you're looking for. All right?"

Suz blinked. "I think you are," she said softly.

He shook his head. "I'm not, darling. I'm just Frog, no matter how much you want to turn me into Cisco, the conquering hero."

He sounded serious, and angry, and almost like he wished she hadn't come. Suz gulped, not about to let him go again, not when she'd come so far to find him. So she kissed him, not the way he'd kissed her, but softly, enticingly, begging him silently to make love to her.

And he seemed to get the message. His eyes widened and she felt his breath catch in his chest, where she'd put a hand over his heart. His muscles felt wonderful, his whole body was wonderful, and when he pulled off her pj top, she hurriedly scooted up against him, gazing up at him with huge eyes. "Fair warning, I really do want a baby."

He studied her. "My baby?"

"Yes." She gasped as he stroked her breasts, kissing her as he did. He shoved down her pj shorts and she moaned against his mouth, which seemed to inflame him. He kissed her hard, urgently, and Suz gasped out, "Cisco, I'm very serious. I'm on that same prescription Mackenzie took—"

"That's nice," he said, interrupting her by taking her mouth with his, exploring it as his hands explored her body and the secret places that were hot and wet for him.

"You're going to kill me," he said. "I'm going to have a massive heart attack if I don't have you."

She was going to expire if he didn't get on with it, so Suz tugged him closer, leaving him no doubt about how much she wanted him. Her hands roamed his body, all the wonderful muscles and strong, hard places—and especially the hardest place of all, which made Cisco groan like a tiger. And when he finally slid inside her, Suz gasped, staring up at him, feeling like a thousand stars were exploding inside her. He played with her, taking her so close to the edge of pleasure, then pulling back just to hear her gasp his name. And beg. She begged him not to leave her, to release her from the pleasure he held back.

When he finally did, magic swept Suz, something she'd never felt before. Cisco held her in his arms, tight, oh, so tight, and her tremors of pleasure forced him over the edge, too.

She closed her eyes, loving being in his arms.

It was the best moment of her life. And she never, ever wanted it to end.

CISCO HAD DIED and gone to heaven, and heaven was a sweet pair of peach-size breasts, a petite woman clinging to him, pressing those darling breasts against his chest, her legs locked around him like she couldn't bear to be parted from him. He closed his eyes tightly, thinking that if this was the prize at the end of any race, he could turn into a regular warrior to stand and fight for this every day.

The thing was, Suz had an agenda. He was going to have to turn her agenda into his. And that would take a lot of work, because she was a product—a favorite daughter—of a very tricky town.

"Okay, beautiful, up and at 'em," he said, carrying her into the shower. "We have a long drive ahead of us." He set her down gently, gazing at her. "God, you're beautiful."

"Where are we going?" Suz asked.

"Back to BC to get some things straightened out. That's why you're here, right?"

"Not entirely."

He turned the water on, making sure it wasn't freezing before he carefully pushed her under it. "Yes, entirely." Now she was all slick and sexy, slick as she'd been in the wet suit in Bridesmaids Creek, only now she was gloriously naked and Cisco realized he'd made a slight miscalculation of how much he wanted her. Her breasts had tipped into delicate peaks, so he had to kiss those, teasing them into tight hardness that drew a moan from her. Of course he had to kiss her again, catch those moans with his mouth. Then he had to kiss a path from her waist down to those heart-shaped butt cheeks, and kissing them led him around to her sweetness. When she clutched his hair and gasped his name, Cisco teased her into pleasure he wanted her to remember for a long time. He lifted her onto him, holding her, trapping her against him so he could let her ride him to her heart's content.

When she cried out his name, he relaxed into his own pleasure, loving the fact that he was buried deep inside her. He kissed her neck and then her lips urgently, wanting so badly to tell her that this was the magic, this was the charm. No charm or magic back in BC could predict this much rightness, this much passion.

He had to make his point, which couldn't be made in a shower. Switching off the water, he dried her off and carried her to the bed, looking forward to spending all day in the sheets with her—after he rode the bull he was scheduled to master today.

"I'm going back with you," Cisco said against her lips, "but you have to marry me."

Chapter Six

Suz froze at Cisco's words. "*Marry* you?"

He didn't look like he was going to take back his statement, which sounded like something a man might say in the heat of passion. "Yes. Marry me. Before we go back to BC. We'll drive to Las Vegas, and we'll do it. In secret." He kissed the tip of her nose, stroked a nipple into hardness, convincing her that he was serious. "That secret thing we're rumored to have sounds pretty good to me."

Suz pulled back, tugged the covers up over her to keep Cisco on task. "Someone has to talk sense, and apparently it's not going to be you. If you're going back to BC, you're planning to run in the race next weekend."

He nodded. "Absolutely. I'm all about the fundraising, because underneath everything, I think that helps BC the most."

"But it won't be an honest run. You won't be a true candidate for marriage."

He kissed her, and Suz squirmed, wishing they could lie in this bed and kiss for another week.

"It's our secret thing, babe."

Suz shook her head. "I'm certain no one has ever tried to cheat the magic before, Cisco."

"Ah, but we were. You were suggesting that I throw the race to my buddy Squint. I'm willing to do that." He kissed her again, and she couldn't help arching up against him, trying to get more of his mouth. "But," he said, "I want what I came to Bridesmaids Creek for in return. And as you may recall, when Ty Spurlock talked us into coming here, he said BC was ripe with ladies who wanted nothing more than to become brides. 'To experience the magic of BC for themselves,' he said, 'with their own big day.'" He tugged her fanny up against him, fitting her to him. "As far as I'm concerned, I've competed for you twice. I'm going to do it a third time, at the cost to my pride, but I'll lose the race to win my bride."

Suz swallowed. "That's quite poetic. I don't think I realized you wanted to get married that badly."

"I didn't. Not until I met you. Frankly, I thought Ty was full of crap. I came along for the ride." He teased her with the promise of future pleasure, then playfully spanked her bottom. "Let's go get married. Then I'll reward you with the best lovemaking you've ever experienced in your life, I promise you."

Suz's head swam. "I thought you already had."

He laughed, got out of bed and slid on his jeans. "Appetizer. Just enough to get you interested."

She was interested, all right. Suz hopped out of bed and dressed in a hurry. "I'm a little worried about this scheme you've cooked up. It feels like it has a few holes."

"Don't worry about anything. We'll get married, and then sometime this summer, we'll get married again, for public digestion. I'm sure you want a Bridesmaids Creek shindig with all the trimmings."

"I never thought about it." Suz gave her hair a flip, then slowly reached to take out the piercings. She studied herself in the bath mirror, a little transfixed by how different she looked without them.

"What are you doing?"

"Going a little more traditional."

"Don't do it on my behalf. I think you're beautiful just the way you are." Cisco tossed some things into his duffel.

"Are you still riding?"

He straightened. "I'm getting married tonight. I'll be on my honeymoon, won't I?"

She blinked. "Honeymoon?"

"We can come back here, or we can stay in Vegas. Whatever you like. You're the bride, it's your big day. Secretly."

"This is silly. You should be resting."

"Here's the deal, gorgeous. Either I ride that bull, or I honeymoon with my new bride. Take your choice."

Suz didn't have to think long. "Will you regret terribly giving up the circuit?"

"I didn't say I was giving it up. I'll be back."

She stared at him. "So our secret thing is going to be so secret that we live in two different places?"

He shrugged. "I can't exactly shack up with you in BC, can I? Folks would figure things out pretty quick. They're not exactly slow around there, you know."

All the air went out of Suz. "I guess you're right."

"Anyway, wasn't the purpose of this to get Daisy off your and Mackenzie's necks, so that she'll stop the foreclosure on your addition for the haunted house?"

"Yes, but—"

"So when I'm in town I'll live in the bunkhouse with

the guys, the way I always have. Daisy will turn her sights on Squint, and I won't be around for her to concentrate on. She'll forget all about me, and John Squint Mathison can be the big cheese."

Suz sank onto the bed. "I'm a little nervous."

"I know how to get rid of your nerves." He grinned at her, quite devilishly sure of himself.

She couldn't help thinking about bulls stomping all over her surprise fiancé. "Is there anything else you could do besides ride bulls? Maybe pass out cotton candy or run the calf catch on the rodeo circuit?"

He picked up her duffel. "Come on, cupcake. You don't strike me as the kind of lady who has trouble making up her mind."

"I know. But I wasn't expecting to be proposed to. I'm trying to think through your scheme," she said, a bit breathlessly. "I've heard a lot of scheming in BC—I grew up on it—but I don't think I was expecting you to be able to operate in that gear."

He nodded toward the door. "You're going to be the cutest little bride BC has ever seen."

"Only they won't know."

"Not yet. No rocking the Daisy boat if we're going to save your haunted house and your family home."

"I guess you're right." Suz gulped. "Didn't you think you'd have to be in love to get married?"

He opened the door. "Come on. I'll carry you over the threshold on our way out."

Of course she wanted to marry Cisco. He was the man of her dreams. She just wasn't certain he wasn't doing all this to be the prince of the fairy tale. Eventually, they'd have to settle into a house, a marriage under one roof—and then what? Cisco didn't know anything about her. She knew very little about him.

On the other hand, getting married this way was very romantic. It appealed to her wild side, the part of her heart that had sent her to remote locations.

And it would keep him off that stupid bull—at least give him some time to recover before he got on another one.

"I can see your brain working," Cisco said, "and I promise you, I intend for our honeymoon to be every bit as energetic as riding that bull would be, so don't think you're keeping me safe. In fact, our honeymoon is going to go a whole lot longer than eight seconds, gorgeous."

She swallowed. Who could pass that up?

Not me.

It sounded like heaven.

"No Elvis ceremony," Suz said, sweeping past him. "I'm a traditional girl."

Cisco laughed.

"WE GOT MARRIED in secret," Suz told Mackenzie, unable to keep her news from her only close living relative. Who didn't tell their sister they'd gotten married?

Mackenzie gasped. "You married *Frog*?"

"*Cisco*. And yes, I did. In Vegas, last weekend." She grinned, unable to help herself. Cisco had been so very sweet to her, made the occasion so special. Had even bought her what he called a secret wedding ring, with lots of turquoise and opals, that was absolutely lovely. He promised to buy her a traditional diamond later— but she'd told him no, thank you. The ring he'd given her was perfect.

Mackenzie hugged her. "I can't believe my baby sister is married!"

"Top secret, though, Mack," Suz warned. "You can't tell a soul."

"Oh, I won't." Mackenzie hugged her again. "It doesn't seem real because I didn't see it with my own eyes." She got a little misty. "To be honest, I've been dreaming of your wedding day for a long time. I always envisioned us together on that day."

"We're having a traditional wedding this summer," Suz said, soothing her. "I promise, it'll be wonderful and traditional."

"I'm just so glad you're happy." Mackenzie glanced toward the mantel where photos of their parents, and happy occasions with them, reminded them of childhood memories. "Mom and Dad would be so proud."

"Yes, they would. They know we've been fighting the good fight. We'll keep the Hanging H if it's the last thing we do." Suz was certain of that. Cisco's plan was as airtight as any plan could be. He was on her side—the Hawthorne side—and everything would work out just fine.

It had to.

THE PLANS CAREFULLY LAID, Cisco went to the starting line for the Best Man's Fork run—though technically, he wasn't a best man. Hadn't been a best man for Justin's wedding, or Ty's. In fact, he was already a groom.

But this was the way life happened in BC, and he was willing to run the race if it meant freeing them from the past. Most important, freeing him of Daisy.

He took a deep breath as John Squint Mathison and

Sam lined up next to him, along with Daisy's five ruffians.

"We're going to win," Carson Dare said, "we're going to beat you."

"I doubt it." If there was going to be smack-talking, Cisco figured he'd better be enthusiastic about the prize.

"I've got all of you beaten," Squint said, "you should probably go ahead and quit now."

Cisco looked at his buddy. "Didn't you say that about the BC swim, too?"

"I'm not cramping up today." The expression on Squint's face was very serious.

"Take your marks!" Sheriff McAdams called.

The runners all bent down. Cisco was still a bit achy, actually more than a bit achy, thanks to his rodeo escapades—which made him very happy. He could put forth his best effort to satisfy the town that he'd made a maximum good-faith showing, and there would be no further discussion of him and Daisy, thanks to the soreness and misery he still suffered from the stomping he'd taken.

"Best of luck to you, fellows," Cisco said. "May the best man win."

The gun popped, and the runners surged forward. It was a mile run, and Cisco felt fairly confident that if he ran lights-out for about a quarter mile, then slowly began easing off, he'd be passed at least by Squint, and maybe by all the runners.

Ignoring the pain and tearing from his current injuries, Cisco stayed at the head of the pack. They rounded a corner in the trail that wound through a forest of ancient oaks and cottonwood trees. With every pace, his heart became lighter. He was going to be free of Daisy and her silly preoccupation with him, she'd forget about revenge on Suz Hawthorne and the Hanging H, and the town of BC would get much-needed revenue from the daily amusement park that was the Haunted H.

He ran faster, easily outpacing the other runners, lost in his fantasy—until he realized he could see the half-way marker. There should be other runners breathing down his neck—but there was only silence.

Cisco turned to look. There wasn't a soul on the path with him.

"Damn!" He stopped in his tracks, put his hands on his knees, gulping deep breaths and cataloging the various aching body parts. Where the hell was everyone?

He listened, heard nothing.

Something was very wrong. The skin on the back of his neck tightened, warning him. Around the curve in the trail, no doubt he would find the long stretch to the finish line. Behind him, very likely he would find not a single soul.

He'd be willing to bet all of BC was in on this practical joke. Because that's what this had to be—especially since no one knew he was already married to Suz.

And happily married, too. Very happily married.

The only thing to do was to call their bluff. Cisco took off running back down the path toward the starting line. He'd nearly gotten to the first quarter-mile marker when Daisy's gang sprang from behind trees and grabbed him, dragging him off the trail.

"What the hell?" Cisco demanded.

"Run!" they shouted, taking off as fast as they could toward the finish line.

Cisco glanced around, saw Squint tied to a tree. "What are you doing?"

"Waiting on you, obviously. Untie me!" Squint glared at him. "Took you long enough!"

"Where the hell is Sam?" Cisco glanced around.

"Never left the starting line, of course," Squint said, his tone unimpressed. "Never had any intention of doing so. He was just making sure we felt prodded by his presence. No Plan Sam had a plan all along, as usual."

Cisco untied Squint, who took off toward the finish line at top speed. Cisco shook his head, trotted after the group of runners, taking his sweet time because by now there was no point in doing more than coasting. A foul plan was afoot, and he'd find out exactly what had happened at the finish line.

What he found at the finish line was a very angry Daisy Donovan, her gang of five goofballs, and a steamed Squint. "What's going on?" Cisco demanded of everyone grouped around, a very quiet finish line with no cheers and nothing but Daisy's annoyed huffs.

"What happened is that you threw the race," Daisy said, flinging her chocolate locks as she jerked her head toward her gang. "My guys say you and Squint cheated."

"Cheated?" He glanced over at Suz, who looked as puzzled as he did. "*We* cheated?"

"Yes. And you deliberately lost the race!" Daisy pointed at him. "That's a violation of committee rules."

"I'm afraid she's correct." Sheriff McAdams sidled up, a grim expression on his face. "This is an honest race. All these spectators," he said, flinging his arm to indicate the throngs of out-of-towners who'd come to see a bride get her bachelor in a much-anticipated race, "will have to have their entrance fees returned."

He glanced at Suz. Her eyes huge, she looked as

distressed as everyone else. Cisco shrugged. "I didn't cheat. Daisy's gang grabbed Squint and me and held us back so we couldn't compete."

The crowd gasped and murmured nervously. "Is this true?" Sheriff McAdams asked Squint. Cosette Lafleur and Jane Chatham stood beside him as rules committee chairs, their gazes interested.

"No, it's not true," Squint said, and Cisco raised a brow. "I wasn't held back."

"You were tied to a tree!" Cisco glared at his buddy, whom he'd quite rightly expected he could count on for backup.

"My only goal was to win the race." Squint looked at Daisy, longing in his gaze. She didn't seem to register his appeal, since her scorn was laser-focused on Cisco.

Right now he was the villain of the day. He had no one in his corner, and this was a game of which he had no knowledge of the rules. There were teed-off patrons of BC and inhabitants alike who wanted his head for messing up their treasured, revered Best Man's Fork run.

It was, as Ty Spurlock always said, a town that ran on carneys—carnival barkers and shysters sweetly selling their homespun shtick.

"It doesn't matter, folks," he said cheerfully. "You'll have to get your pound of flesh elsewhere. I lost the race, despite giving it my best effort, even after being stomped by a bull last weekend. No one has given more in this race today than me."

Daisy clapped her hands. "I knew it! You do care for me!"

This had to be extinguished now. It couldn't go on another second, not for all the bragging rights in Texas.

"Nope, I don't, Daze. To be honest, I'm already married."

The gasp that met his announcement sounded like stoppers had been pulled out of a thousand bottles. Every single citizen of BC wore a frown of disapproval—but Suz's gaze was the most worried. Discreetly she shook her head—*no, no*—and belatedly Cisco realized that in trying to extract himself from Daisy's net—and the town's unhappiness with him—the Hanging H was on the hook with the Donovans. And it wouldn't help if Daisy learned that he was married to Suz.

Now was not the time to reveal all.

"What exactly do you mean, you're already married, son?" Sheriff McAdams asked.

Cisco shrugged. "I just am."

"I don't believe you," Daisy said.

"It's true." Cisco shrugged again. "I'm a happily married man."

"Ty Spurlock said he was bringing bachelors to save our town," Sheriff McAdams said. "He trusted you to be who you said you were."

Cisco shook his head. "I'm packing up, kids. I ran the race, as I was asked—"

"Three times!" Daisy pointed a finger at him, looking at the crowd for assistance. "He cheated me in three different races!"

This was a matter of debate, as far as Cisco was concerned—but the fact that his buddy deliberately sold him out was of overwhelming concern. "I'll talk to you later," he said to Squint, and got in his truck, uttering a slight groan when his bull-injured body encountered the resistance of the seat. It had been rough running today—but it had all been worth it because he knew how much it meant to Suz.

Suz glanced away when he looked at her, practically pleading with him not to reveal her secret. He wouldn't, not even by going to hug her, no matter how much he was dying to hold her in his arms. This whole mess was in some respects his fault. But she was his wife, and if she wanted to wait awhile to make the big announcement, he was happy to do things her way. After all, this was her town.

As Cisco drove off, he realized he didn't even know who'd won the race. However, it wasn't him, and that made him the happiest cowboy on the planet.

Bridesmaids Creek could have their charms—he believed in doing things the old-fashioned way.

His way.

Chapter Seven

The kitchen at the Hanging H was a lively spot when Cisco made his way there after evening chores. He'd hidden himself on the ranch, taking care of business—doing anything but being in the line of fire after the race that wasn't. By now, he knew everyone would have returned to the evening gathering place, and even though he knew he was in the doghouse, he wanted to see his secret bride too much to stay away.

The kitchen clan, consisting of Mackenzie and Justin, Suz, Squint and Sam, went dead silent when he walked in. He took off his Stetson, looked at all the faces staring at him. "Guys, I did my best. I really did. And anyway, will you please tell me why you weren't honest about Daisy's gang waylaying us?" he demanded of Squint.

Squint shrugged. "I wasn't about to let Daisy down. She's my girl."

"She is *not* your girl!" Cisco felt like he'd fallen down Alice in Wonderland's rabbit hole. "I don't think Daisy knows you're alive, bro."

"She knows now. Because I won." Squint looked really happy about that.

"You won. Yes, you did." Cisco wasn't going to argue

the point, not with Suz standing there looking like a luscious dream he just wanted to get back in his arms. "And I lost. Which is awesome. So you didn't back me up about us being dragged off the race path because you didn't want Daisy's big day ruined?"

Everyone turned to look at Squint. "Well, how do you think she'd feel if she discovered that her winner—the man who is meant to be hers—didn't really want to win?"

Cisco sank onto a bar stool, accepted the cup of coffee and plate of chocolate chip cake Mackenzie handed him. Everyone else received the same, and Cisco dug in, hoping that perhaps food would take some of the edge off what he felt in the room. He couldn't remember ever being this annoyed with his buddies. And he was irritated with both Squint and Sam, if the truth were known. Squint might have been covering up to save Daisy's feelings, but Cisco had a funny feeling Sam was in the plan up to his Handsome Sam neck. His buddy was a trickster, and ever since they'd returned stateside and come to Bridesmaids Creek, Cisco hadn't known if Sam was dealing from the bottom or top of the deck.

Suz stayed on her side of the kitchen island, not giving away their relationship. As far as Cisco was concerned, this was the hardest part of all. He wanted to declare their love to one and all—but he had to act like it was some kind of deep, dark secret.

Which had been his idea, so it was tough cookies for him.

"So why did Daisy's gang tie you to a tree?" Cisco demanded.

Squint shook his head. "At first I thought it was on Daisy's orders, because she'd probably known I could beat you running. Figured she was trying to give you every chance to prove yourself. But then her gang gave me such a tough run—I'm telling you, I barely crossed the finish line in front of them—that I realized something else was going on." Squint took a deep breath, glanced around the room to make certain everyone was listening. "Our resident matchmaker was behind that little stunt."

Suz gasped. "Cosette Lafleur would never!"

"I assure you she did." Squint nodded. "I overheard one of Daisy's knuckleheads mutter something about it when they were standing at the finish line. I have excellent SEAL hearing."

Everyone took a stool to consider this new twist.

"I just find it very hard to believe that Cosette would try to influence the results," Mackenzie said. "She's been our matchmaker forever. I can't remember a match in this town she hasn't had some hand in, either secretly or publicly. And she's on the rules committee."

Suz met Cisco's gaze, moving her head slightly in the negative. Theirs was one wedding that hadn't had Cosette's help—and maybe that was a good thing. He thought his little bride looked a bit guilty that they didn't have the matchmaker's blessing and magic wand waved over their marriage, but he wasn't from BC. He could handle his own love life, and right now, he had exactly what he wanted, which was Suz. Secretly, Suz Grant. He grinned at her and she blushed, which he thought was darling.

Tonight, he was going to make love to her until she blushed all over.

"Well, believe it," Squint said. "No one knows what resources matchmakers utilize to effect matches, I suppose. In this case, she chose to hire Daisy's gang to put Frog and me out of the running long enough for them to win. They had a head start, but I wasn't about to lose that race." He looked at Cisco. "Why did you come back, anyway? You could have kept running and won."

"Because you're my brother," Cisco said, growling. "I'd never leave a brother behind. Never have, never will."

"All right, all right. Stand down." Justin waved both men to cool their jets. "Let's just figure out where we go from here."

Cisco glanced at Suz. His wife smiled at him, her gaze bright. God, he loved her delicate little face. He would have run from end to end of the entire United States if it meant he'd win her. "Why would we go anywhere?"

"Well, some of us might be going somewhere," Sam said, "since apparently one of us is married and didn't share that with any of us." Sam frowned, his face marred by an expression that rarely registered on him. "We served together. I think I'd know if you were married, bro."

Cisco shrugged. "I have a few secrets."

Everyone stared at him, waiting for him to elaborate. "Well, I'm not going to talk about it now. It doesn't change anything about the fact that I want to help BC. Just not as a dedicated bachelor."

"You realize Daisy's really pissed," Justin said. "She thinks she's been gypped of her one true love."

"I leave that to Squint to figure out." Cisco glanced at Suz, couldn't help winking at her. "And I'll pay for all the tickets that had to be refunded."

Mackenzie nodded. "Thank you. That'll go a long

way to soothing town feathers, although not Daisy's. She spent three races hoping you were the one, Cisco."

"Yeah, well, I'm not," he said cheerfully, not looking at Suz just in case someone figured out that he couldn't keep his eyes off his sexy lady. "I'm not Daisy's 'one,' that's for certain."

"She won't get another race," Suz said, "and she's not happy about it."

"Doesn't matter," Squint said bravely. "I won today."

"That's right." Cisco nodded. "After today, everything changes."

A knock on the back door startled everyone. Mackenzie opened the door, and Daisy blew inside, heading straight for Cisco. "You made a laughingstock of my big day, Cisco Grant, and I want you to know that I despise you. I despise all of you!"

Even if he was glad to be out of Daisy's line of fire, she could still hold up the Hanging H's funding. "Daisy, I'm not your guy. You can't be mad about that. There's a better man out there for you."

"Yeah," Squint said. "I did win today."

Daisy looked at him, as if seeing him for the first time. Cisco held his breath, his gaze on Suz.

Then Daisy turned back to him. "The thing is, you cheated, Cisco. I've had three chances at the Bridesmaids Creek magic, and there's not going to be another time for me."

No one in the room spoke up, and since Cisco wasn't versed in BC lore, he kept his mouth shut.

Fire flashed in Daisy's eyes at his silence. "It wasn't that hard to check up on your claim that you're married. Turns out, you really are."

Suz looked frozen in place. He desperately wanted

to put his arms around her, tell her it was going to be all right. "Yeah, well, a man doesn't usually make up the M word, Daze."

Daisy looked around the room, her gaze settling on Suz. "Private investigators are easy to hire. It wasn't a secret that was going to keep. Everybody knows there really aren't secrets in BC."

"So, Daisy," Sam said, "stop killing us with the suspense. If you think my buddy here is married, who dragged him to the altar?"

Daisy's eyes darkened with anger. "He married Suz last weekend. Which I should have seen coming, because honestly, the Hawthorne sisters will do anything they possibly can to make sure my father and I never belong in this town."

SUZ STOOD STRAIGHTER, her back immediately up as Daisy made her announcement. Every pair of eyes in the room landed on her in astonishment, before traveling to Cisco, who grinned, not minding the spotlight at all. Suz shook her head. "I didn't do anything to cheat you, Daisy. I don't know what happened at the Best Man's Fork run. It sounds like your gang was up to their ears in mischief, as usual, so you can't lay that at my door." She took a deep breath, her gaze going to Cisco. He smiled at her, tall and dark and handsome as always. He was sweet, but the man didn't understand Daisy, he didn't understand the workings of BC, and frankly, she was too nervous to return his smile. "Your dream guy is still out there, somewhere."

"Yeah," Squint said, "you didn't want my buddy Frog Legs, anyway."

Cisco laughed, not minding the razzing one bit. "She

may not want a one-eyed squinter, either. Even if he can shoot the label off a beer bottle at a very distant range, which is how he got the name Squint. Not a bad talent in a man, you know."

"That's all very well and good," Daisy snapped, "but the fact remains, my big day has been stolen from me." She looked at Suz, and Suz could feel her fury. "You and your sister have been queen bees ever since I came to this town. It's time you learn that other people have feelings, too."

"Come on, Daisy. No one can help who they fall in love with. And you're not in love with Cisco." Suz was certain of this. Daisy had latched on to Cisco for some reason, but she wasn't sure what. "I'm sorry we kept our marriage from you, and from everyone else, too," she said, glancing around the room. "But actually, we wanted you to have your big day."

"So my father will stop the proceedings against your addition for the Haunted H." Daisy tossed her hair. "That's not going to happen. Better still, it turns out that you took a lien against the Hanging H for your haunted house business. Which means," Daisy said triumphantly, "that before too long, this house, the ranch and your business will be owned by Donovan Enterprises. Better known as me."

Suz couldn't bear the stricken look on her sister's face. Her own heart felt like it was tearing in two. "Daisy, I'm sure we can work this out. If you want a husband, there are lots of men who would want to marry you, I'm sure. You just have to be patient with the magic."

"Yeah?" Daisy went to the door. "I intend to make my own magic from now on. Not silly, manufactured Bridesmaids Creek magic that seems to work for everyone but me. Anyway, all that crap is just that—crap. There's no magic in this town. It's just a pile of old, dusty buildings and elderly folk trying to hold on to the past. And you and your sister and Jade Harper trying to become the next team of biddies running the BC show. I don't care," Daisy said. "I'm going to be the BC queen bee from now on. Enjoy house hunting, Suz."

She went out the door, and Suz sank onto a bar stool. Mackenzie put her arms around her sister. A second later, she felt Cisco's big warm hand on her shoulder, too.

"I guess congratulations are in order," Sam said, trying to kick-start some joy in the kitchen that felt peculiarly like all the happiness had evaporated.

"Indeed," Squint said. "Let's have some cake to celebrate our newly married couple!"

No one joined in his idea. Suz and Mackenzie sat together like a still-life painting.

"Do you think she means it?" Mackenzie asked.

"Of course she means it," Suz answered. "Daisy feels like we made her a laughingstock. The worst part is, I can actually see her point."

"Hey!" Cisco sat on the stool next to her, smoothed her hair back from her face. "Marrying you was the happiest moment of my life. I'm still in awe that I landed such an amazing woman."

"Me, too," Sam said, his mouth full of cake. "So is everyone else. The question is, what are we going to do to fix this problem?"

Suz could hardly wrap her mind around what had just happened. "I can live anywhere. I've lived in lots of remote locations with bare minimum comforts. But Mackenzie has four babies." She looked at her sister.

"I'm so sorry, Mackenzie. I didn't think what my marriage might do to you."

"Hey!" Cisco took her hand. "Let's not make it sound like we've done something we shouldn't have."

Suz shook her head. "I should have known better. I didn't consult Madame Matchmaker, and I cheated our system here. Even Ty remembered to respect the town when he won Jade's heart. I was thinking about having a baby, and being a wife."

"I'm still trying to figure out how our town matchmaker comes to tie people up to effect her matchmaking credentials," Sam said, cutting himself another slice of cake. "This is a wacky little town."

"I don't think Daisy's ever going to have me." Squint looked around the room. "I don't even think she knows my name."

Suz took a deep breath. "Daisy's too mad right now. And honestly, I don't blame her a bit." She got up, hugged her sister. "Somehow we'll find a way to undo this. It's my mistake, and I'll figure it out."

She took herself up to her room, feeling like she'd let everyone in BC down—including her new husband.

She hadn't thought this through, that much was clear. Her fast, secret marriage had been an impetuous mistake. She'd hurt her sister and her family, the townspeople and BC, too. Why? Because she'd fallen for Cisco.

He didn't even know that she'd hurt him, too.

Chapter Eight

"Hey, little lady!" Cisco said, following his wife into her room. "You and I are meant to be, beautiful. I don't want to hear you rethinking what we did and I definitely heard you rethinking it downstairs. I want that train of thought stopped. Immediately." He took Suz in his arms, kissing her, holding her the way he'd been dying to ever since Daisy's unfortunate entrance.

Suz pulled from his arms. "You don't understand, Cisco."

She sat on the end of her bed, and he sat next to her, taking in the rose-patterned drapes and white bedspread, white furniture and girlie accoutrements at a glance. "Explain it to me."

"Remember when I told you I was taking medication to help me get pregnant?"

"Dimly. Very dimly. I'm pretty sure I was in the throes of passion and wasn't listening to the fine details." He took a deep breath. "My God, Suz, I had you naked in my arms. You could have told me you were playing on Daisy's team and I doubt it would have registered."

"That makes it even worse, then. I should have made sure you were listening."

"Okay, I'm listening now. I'm all ears. Get it all off your chest." Cisco didn't touch his wife, recognizing that Daisy's visit had upset her far more deeply than he'd realized—and the fact that she was clearly so devastated was killing him.

Suz took a deep breath. "I'm on the same medication Mackenzie was taking because the chances of me being able to conceive are very low. My sister and I have some similar issues."

"Clearly it doesn't matter. She's got four. I'm pretty sure I can duplicate some success in that department. Considering how much I adore your body, I'm looking forward to the challenge." He tweaked her hair, trying to rouse a smile from her.

"And if I can't get pregnant?"

He shrugged. "So? I married you, not your ovaries."

They sat silently for a few minutes. Cisco struggled to think how he could explain his feelings to Suz better, set her free from whatever was bugging her. "Listen, I had a bunch of good buddies who didn't get to come home to their families, Suz. Their wives, their children. It's real hard for me to sit around and cry about what might or might not happen with pregnancy in our marriage."

"I needed to hear that," Suz murmured.

"All right, then. Let's not sell me short just yet, beautiful. I may not be the Prince Charming BC was looking for, but I'm probably pretty close," he said cheerfully, feeling confident about that.

"Cisco," Suz said, looking into his eyes, "you're going to have to leave BC."

He stopped cold, something strange seeping into his chest at the serious look in her eyes and the tone in her voice. "I'm not going anywhere without you, babe. I know we said we'd live apart, but now that our secret's out, I'm going to be an attentive husband. That's how we're going to achieve that pregnancy you're hoping for."

Suz's shoulders slumped a bit. "You're going to have to give me some time to sort this out. And you being here is just going to make Daisy mad on a daily basis. A sore that isn't going to heal."

He got it. Daisy definitely believed that they'd married secretly to rig the charity run—and she was right. But he could have run a thousand races and it wouldn't have mattered. BC didn't have enough charms, powerful enough charms, to make him love anyone but Suz. She was the woman of his heart. He felt like he'd come to BC just to find her, as if she'd been waiting for him.

Or maybe his heart had been waiting for her.

"Whatever I have to do to win you for good, I'll do it." Cisco wrapped his arms around her as they lay on the bed together. "I don't pretend to be wise in the ways of BC. I don't understand a town whose supposed matchmaker cheats with the best of them." He still felt outraged about that incident on the trail, but since he hadn't "won" the race—by BC standards, anyway, though it was still a win in his book, a reverse win—he wasn't going to probe too deeply into Madame Matchmaker's machinations. "I can go away for a week or two."

Suz rolled up onto his chest, gazed down into his eyes. "I'm thinking longer. Memories are healthy here in BC. And if I have any prayer of Daisy cooling off and deciding not to take our house and our land, she needs to not be reminded daily that she feels like we made her a laughingstock."

"I guess we kind of did." He didn't want to, but he could see Daisy's side. A little.

"Actually, she's not too far off when she says BC never really embraced her and her family. We never went out of our way to invite her to things. I hate to say it, but I think on that she's right. It wasn't that we were trying to be mean. Daisy just didn't fit in BC. Her father was loud and rude, rubbed everyone the wrong way. It colored our feelings about Daisy."

He could see how that had happened. "I haven't seen any overt sign that folks look down on Daisy since I came to BC. I do see that she and Robert are pretty unlikable characters."

"But I think she was trying to change." Suz looked at him. "I honestly believe she was making an effort. After we started inviting her around here more, she seemed to be trying to get along better. I feel bad about that."

"Let's beat ourselves up about one thing at a time. Right now, we have to deal with the major problem, which is that apparently Robert owns the bank that has your note? Did I understand that correctly?"

"If not Robert, then his cronies. Remember, he's been buying up BC land and buildings and offering them to government entities."

"Yeah, but I thought Jade made Robert promise he wouldn't levy any further action against the people of this town, especially if he wanted to see his grandchildren. Supposedly everything changed when Robert found out that Ty Spurlock was his son, and when he and Jade had children. Didn't it soften Daisy up, too, becoming an aunt?"

"I'm guessing Daisy thinks we cheated her, so all past promises are off." Suz's eyes were sad. "I knew better than to do what we did, Cisco. Nothing that happens in secret is probably ever going to turn out optimally."

An arrow of pain shot into his heart. "You don't regret marrying me, do you?"

"I don't regret marrying you, but I wish we'd taken other people's feelings into account. Even my sister was a little hurt that we didn't have a traditional wedding she could attend. And I totally understand."

"We agreed we'd have a regular wedding later. And that there'd be no secrets kept between us. I'm still good for that on my end, doll."

Yet no matter how much he wanted to fix the situation for Suz, Cisco also knew that hurt feelings and broken promises weren't mended overnight.

In fact, healing took a long, long time.

A WEEK LATER, Suz sat in Cosette's office in the cozy tearoom-like atmosphere of Madame Matchmaker's Premiere Matchmaking Services. A floral teapot graced a small coffee table between the flowered chairs, inviting conversation. Cosette gazed at her, her pink-frosted hair somehow looking completely perfect in the delicate room.

"So you found yourself in a dilemma," Cosette said. "I hate to see it, of course. Our town prides itself on romance done properly."

Suz looked at her longtime friend. "Cosette, I need your advice."

"Of course you do, dear. That's what I'm here for," she said in her lovely French-accented voice. "Tell me everything."

"My husband left BC." Suz took a deep breath. "We decided it was for the best."

"So I heard." Cosette shook her head. "Very sad situation. Marriages that don't start off on the right foot can be tricky."

"I want my marriage to work out, Cosette. I want it to lose the tricky flavor."

"All right." Cosette poured out tea. "How long is Cisco planning to be gone?"

"As long as it takes for Daisy to cool off."

Cosette gave her a sidelong glance. "That could be never."

"So I need to arrange a match for Daisy." Suz felt that was the best avenue of action. "I feel that I owe it to her."

"Why?" Cosette dropped two sugar cubes into their teacups and stirred hers, seeming untroubled by Suz's plan.

"Because it's true that Cisco and I got married and didn't tell anyone. It seemed like the right thing to do at the time, but obviously it wasn't." She took a deep breath. "I feel bad for Daisy."

"And possibly your marriage may suffer because you weren't up front from the beginning."

Suz nodded. "I just wanted Cisco so much."

"And you didn't want to take a chance that the magic might work." Cosette shrugged. "Because you might have lost him to Daisy, if he'd been the man intended for her."

"Not really. Cisco and Daisy weren't a match, with or without me. Or magic."

Cosette looked at her, her eyes huge.

"Okay," Suz said. "It's true I didn't trust the magic."

Cosette nodded. "I think that much is clear. And so it backfired on you."

"Which is why I'm here." Suz sipped her tea. "The only way to undo what I did is to make sure that Daisy gets her own match."

"There are no guarantees. It doesn't mean she won't foreclose on the Hanging H. Or on our shops, either. It doesn't mean she'll ever forgive you," Cosette warned. "And it doesn't mean that your marriage is saved."

Suz gulped. "Saved? My marriage is going to be fine."

"Isn't that why you're here? To save it?"

She nodded, surrendering. "I have to try. Doing nothing isn't going to undo any of the damage."

"Are you doing it for the ranch, BC or yourself?"

"All." Suz swallowed, thinking about Cisco. He'd been so disappointed, though he'd agreed it would be better for him to leave BC. The rodeo circuit had been the natural place for him to return, which gave Suz lots of long nights. Seeing your man get stomped by a bull once was a certain way to lose a lot of sleep. "Believe me, I'm not trying to say I'm totally unselfish here. But in the end, I know I caused a lot of people to suffer, and I want to try to fix that."

Cosette nodded. "All right, then."

"But I do have a question." Suz sat up. "Why did you have Squint dragged off the Best Man's Fork trail by Daisy's gang? Were you trying to make Daisy happy so she wouldn't take your and Phillipe's shops?"

"I did it because Daisy asked for my help."

Suz blinked. "*Daisy* asked for your help?"

Cosette nodded. "Sat in that very chair you're sitting in."

Suz scrunched her eyes shut tightly for a second, thinking. She opened them when daylight hit. "Daisy asked you to help her with a match!"

"Yes."

"Did she ask you to have her guys waylay Squint?"

"She said she wanted to make certain that the right man won the race. She wanted to know beyond a shadow of a doubt that the man who could love her in spite of her Donovan roots was the one who won." Cosette put down her teacup and gazed at Suz.

"But they dragged Squint off. That left only Cisco to win the race. And Daisy's gang," Suz said, her voice trailing off as she stared at Cosette. "Did you want Cisco to win?"

"I had nothing to do with the magic. The magic moves itself. You have to understand how these things work in BC. People often manifest their own magic, their own hopes and dreams, either by prayer, fervent hoping—wishing—or focusing on their goals. These things are all possible. It's not woo-woo stuff." Cosette picked up a pink-edged cookie, nibbled at it. "All I did was tell Daisy's gang that whoever won the race that day was going to marry Daisy. Whatever happened after that was beyond anything of my powers. Er, control."

"Like the time Justin won Mackenzie. And Ty won the race for Jade."

"Exactly. Magic can't be cheated."

"Did you know Cisco would go back for Squint? That he wouldn't win the race?" Suz hated to think of what might have happened if Cisco had sprinted on to the finish line. He was a competitive guy—he might have.

Thankfully, he'd cared about his brother-in-arms more than winning.

"I knew nothing, except that the right man would win." She gave a delicate shrug. "I believe he did."

"Is Squint Daisy's true love?"

"Time will tell."

Suz shook her head. "I'd feel better if you arranged a match for Daisy. I don't know if I can rely on magic that may have backfired. There were too many people with their own agendas that day, including me."

Cosette laughed, a cheery sound in the small room. "You want to hire me to make a match for Daisy to clear your conscience, dear. You're going to have to do that all on your own."

"It just doesn't explain why Daisy did, in fact, win Cisco the first two times." She took a deep breath. "There's nothing you can do?" Suz wasn't sure that the matchmaker wasn't being slightly uncooperative in her darling Cosette way.

"The better thing to do might be to make a match for her father, Robert Donovan," Cosette said, smiling mysteriously as she sipped her tea, and Suz gasped.

"Can you do that?"

Cosette looked slightly irritated. "I'm a matchmaker, *ma petite*! Don't be silly!"

Suz thought fast. Could she trust Cosette, who'd been known to thrown a curveball into matters from time to time? Things always worked out in the end, but it was the beginning and middle where matters got tricky. Suz tried to see Robert happily settled, and failed dismally. No one would want the curmudgeonly man.

Suz shook her head. "What do I have to do to help your magic wand work its magic?"

Cosette shuddered. "Ugh, don't speak of such pedantic things. Magic wands indeed. Just because I'm a romantic does not mean that particular Cinderella fairy tale is how I run my business. I don't do magic tricks, either. These young kids," Cosette muttered, puttering off into her shop. "They think everything is done the old-fashioned way. Like genies steam out of my teapot or something."

Suz stared after her friend, realizing she'd been dismissed. It was all in Cosette's hands now, for better or worse.

Suz shivered a little as a strange feeling of something hit her. She put a hand over her mouth for a second, wondering why she all of a sudden felt so off.

It was this shop, with its dainty decor and potpourri and tea smells.

She hurried out into the bright sunlight of the cold February day, feeling very much like something had just shifted precariously in her life.

"You're pregnant," the doctor told Suz a week later, on Valentine's Day, smiling hugely. She hadn't felt right since that day in Cosette's parlor, and could no longer wonder if perhaps a cookie hadn't set right with her.

Mornings had been really bad.

Suz shook her head at the doctor's pronouncement. "I can't be pregnant."

"You are." She looked at the test results. "Confirmed by blood *and* urine tests."

A soft glow shone on Suz's world, suddenly lifting the dark clouds away that had been hovering ever since the night she and Cisco had unceremoniously announced their marriage. "I'm pregnant," she murmured. "I'm pregnant!"

The doctor nodded. "Yes. I'll see you in another

month to check your progress, but for now, I want you to start taking prenatal vitamins. Congratulations to you and Mr. Grant."

Mr. Grant. Suz started.

She went home, trying to decide how best to tell Mr. Grant. It was a wonderful, wonderful Valentine surprise they'd gotten. Suz smiled, putting a hand on her stomach as she did.

The smile faded. If Cisco knew she was pregnant, he'd come barreling home. He would never agree to being away from her. But she had support here with her sister, Jade and her mother, Betty, and all their friends. The best thing for now would be to let Daisy cool off—and hopefully, a cooled-off Daisy might mean she'd relent about taking Cosette and Phillipe's shops, not to mention her own family home.

This was one secret she had to keep.

Chapter Nine

Cisco lay in bed in Montana, staring at the ceiling, pondering the small, spare bunkhouse room he'd been given by the cantankerous owner of the Triple W ranch, Branch Winter. Branch was his age, but didn't care for rodeo. Didn't care for much of anything. Lived on his own out here in the middle of the Montana ranch land, silhouetted by beautiful purple-hued mountains that seemed almost unreal if you were used to the flatter land of Texas.

Which Cisco was. He missed BC, he missed the hell out of his wife. It had been a long seven months without her.

Suz took up a lot of space in his brain. He wondered for the thousandth time if they could have done things better than they had. Impulsive sure hadn't played well in BC—and he'd known it was risky business tinkering with the town traditions. Maybe he was selfish. "So what if I jumped the gun by asking Suz to marry me," he muttered, staring at the rough wood beams in the ceiling. Could anyone blame him? Suz was the kind of woman you grabbed at the first opportunity, and one thing he'd learned very well over the years, Opportunity was a selfish witch. Opportunity gave out her chances very sparingly. In retrospect, he probably *had* jumped the gun by convincing Suz to marry him. The fact that the odds were long against his secret marriage idea hadn't been all that much of a surprise.

The thing was, he'd wanted her so badly. "Go ahead and pour Selfish Bastard Sauce all over me, because I don't have a single regret," he assured the ghosts of regret he figured were probably hanging around somewhere.

Seven months away from her was too damn long. He was in his own personal exile, his personal hell, all because the woman of his dreams came from a little town with big expectations of how life was supposed to run.

Lying low sucked.

But he understood why he was here, and he was determined to show Suz that he could live up to the challenge. If his absence made his marriage stronger because it got Daisy off everyone's backs—and if it meant Suz and he could have a normal marriage, and if it meant Daisy forgave Suz and decided not to foreclose on the Hanging H, exile would have been worth it. The heaping of Selfish Bastard Sauce would have been worth it. He'd go home a hero. What man didn't want to be a conquering warrior?

But every time he'd talked to Suz on the phone, it sounded like matters hadn't cooled off a bit back in BC-town. Cosette and Phillipe had lost their shops, and a divorce quickly followed. They now lived at opposite ends of the town, which was all very awkward for the town denizens. Madame Matchmaker had tried fixing up Robert Donovan, which hadn't gone swimmingly, if the pun could be used. Madame was convinced her magic had deserted her for good. Between the missing magic and the loss of her shop, Suz said Cosette was truly down in the dumps. She didn't show up in town very often, preferred to lie low. He of all people knew how much lying low sucked, because he was low from lying low. Not that he was the complaining type, but he was ready to ride high again.

He was especially low because he'd gotten the daylights stomped out of him, which was why he was convalescing here at Branch's place. He hadn't told Suz because she'd flip out. His little darling was quite sensitive about these types of things, and since this time he'd actually broken a few ribs, Suz would really protest him bull riding. Probably consign him to the kiddie calf catch. There were some secrets a man had to keep, right?

Cisco stared at the red-checked curtains flapping in the breeze. He'd opened his window to get some air, cool as it was outside. The coolness kept him alive, because he was starting to molder from lack of activity. Lying in bed in black boxer shorts, as he had for the past three days, only getting up to shower and eat, was driving him crazy.

Chances were pretty good he'd turn into the abominable snowman before he was back in his wife's arms. If he was lucky, he'd be invited home for Christmas.

Snowmen. Santa would take over the haunted house in December, turning it into Winter Wonderland.

And I'll be the grouchiest, most abominable, love-starved snowman in history.

A knock on his bedroom door startled him. "Door's open!"

Maybe Branch had come to visit him. Not that Branch did that much—he was far too busy, and far too independent to do much socializing. But he'd proven himself a friend once again by giving him shelter, so Cisco sat up, trying to look sociable.

His jaw dropped when Daisy Donovan walked in like his worst catsuited, sexy-as-fire nightmare. "Daisy! What the hell?"

"You are not easy to find, Frog Grant," she said. She'd tied her dark hair into a long ponytail that swept over one shoulder as she flounced over to the only chair in his room, sitting down and making herself far too comfortable. He could feel sweat breaking out all over him.

This was bad. Very bad. Hellish, in fact.

"You shouldn't be here," Cisco stated. If the gossips back in BC got wind of this—and he'd bet a year of pay that's what Daisy intended—there'd be trouble in Paradise.

"How did you find me?"

Daisy smiled. "Sam told me, eventually."

Of course. Handsome Sam, his dear friend who could always be trusted to throw a wrench into matters. Cisco cursed Handsome Sam and wished for a wart the size of a quarter to grace his buddy's nose. "Whatever you want, a phone call would have sufficed."

"There's nothing like being up close and personal, is there?"

Oh, God, she was after him. Planning something devilish. Clearly she hadn't forgiven him, not one whit—as Suz had warned. Suz had said Daisy was still a ball of fire, and there was no good reason to return while the fire was still flaming.

He creaked out of bed, tugged on a T-shirt, wondered

what the hell he'd done with his jeans. "Daisy, you have to leave. Now."

"Not until I say what I've come to say. And you're hurt!"

"No. Not a bit." He was lying like a rug, but, with his luck, Daisy would nominate herself his nurse and then there'd be all kinds of hell to pay. "I'm fine. Say whatever's on your mind and toodle on. I've got to get to work."

She approached, putting a gentle hand on his ribs. "You *are* hurt. That's why you're standing up like an old man."

"Everything's fine." He backed away from the soft hand, putting a couple feet between them as he went to his door. "Out you go."

"Suz is pregnant," Daisy said, and his world dropped to his feet.

"What?"

"Suz, your darling wife," she said, her voice taking on a little edge, "is expecting. Didn't she tell you?"

He gulped. Felt a little more sweat break out all over him, and a case of chills. "Ah, sure she did." Daisy was here on a mission, and she was searching for his weakness, like any good enemy combatant. He wasn't going to show her his weak flank—which was that clearly his little wife was keeping secrets from him.

Daisy would take that to mean their marriage wasn't all that rock-solid, and would begin to brew trouble. "Sure she told me."

Daisy laughed. "I know you didn't know, Frog. The question is, why has Suz been keeping you on the road? The Hawthorne sisters are always plotting, they always have a plan." She went back to the chair, which made him breathe a lot more easily, and seated herself with a teasing, delighted smile. "And not just one baby, either."

Chills hit him, very much like when he'd been wounded, chills that swept all over him. "I know all this, Daisy. You're not telling me anything new."

Daisy looked at her elegant hands, studied her fingernails, drawing out the moment. "It's crazy that Mackenzie had quadruplets and Suz is, too. Who would have thought it could happen twice in one family?"

And with that, he hit the floor.

WHEN CISCO CAME TO, he was lying across his bed. Daisy was next to him, undressed down to a pink lacy see-through bra and a matching thong that showcased way too much of her long, fit body. His head instantly cleared and he jackknifed out of the bed. "Daisy! What the hell?"

She laughed. Put her clothes on. "That was fun. We should do it again some time."

His throat dried out. He watched her walk to the door, his heart hammering. The enemy had scored on him, he knew it; he just didn't know how. He realized his T-shirt had somehow left his body. His blood went colder than winter.

"We didn't do anything," Cisco stated. "Now get out."

Daisy stood in the doorway, tossed her hair. "Call me," she said, blowing him a kiss, waiting for his reaction.

Of course she was insinuating they'd been intimate—but he could have been out of his mind on a bender and he wouldn't have touched Daisy. He was pretty certain parts of his body would shrivel up and

fall off if that ever happened, and not just from BC voodoo. Magic, whatever. He found his jeans where they'd
somehow ended up under the bed and dressed quickly,
his head swimming, as she posed in the door obviously
expecting him to say adios. Or catch the stupid kiss
she'd blown, or something.

What the hell had she done to him?

Quadruplets. Oh, God.

He started to ask her if he was really going to be
a father of four, then swallowed the question, realizing that would play right into her hands. Patience and
courtesy be damned, he shoved her from his room and
locked the door.

Damn it, I'm in trouble.

Cisco glanced at the bed, thinking about Daisy
wrapped around him like some kind of pink-panty-
wearing boa constrictor.

And then it hit him. She'd taken photos, of course.

He tore the bedroom door open, not surprised that
she was still standing there. "Give me your phone."

"Now, Cisco," Daisy said, turning to walk away.
"You don't think I'm the kind of girl who kisses and
tells, do you?"

Crap—she'd kissed him, and taken a selfie. And
he'd been out stupid, poleaxed by the news of quadruplets—which would no doubt look like he was either
in the throes of passion or out cold after lovemaking.
The hammering dance his heart was doing increased.
He let her go, realizing she'd already sent whatever
photos she'd taken.

He was doomed.

As far as he was concerned, BC wasn't about the
fairy tales, happy endings and magic moments. He'd

never experienced any of those in Bridesmaids Creek, not a one. All those purported charms seemed to conspire to work against him. Unlike Ty and Justin, the BC thing just didn't want to give him a break.

Daisy had won him three times fair and square, and she hadn't given up.

Cisco came tearing through the door, nearly giving Suz heart failure. "Cisco!"

He hurried to her side, flinging a bouquet of flowers he'd brought to the floor and dropping to his knees by the side of the chaise on which she was ensconced. By the wild look in her husband's eyes he was very well aware she was pregnant.

"Don't be upset—" she began.

"The whole thing was a crock," Cisco said, his gaze glued to her stomach before raising back up to her face. "It was a crock, and God, I missed you. I've got to kiss you right now."

He did kiss her, and Suz's heart melted. "We should talk," she said, pulling back. Guilt swamped her as she desperately wished she'd been honest with him before someone had informed him of her pregnancy.

"You're darned right." He put a hand on her big round stomach, which these days felt like a baby elephant was in a tent inside her. "I'll go first. No, you. Hell, I don't care. Whatever you want."

He was more handsome than she'd even remembered. As much as she'd missed him, talking to him on a cell phone just didn't cut it. "Cisco—"

"I wasn't with Daisy," he said.

"I know that!"

He let out a long breath. "Feels great to get that off my chest."

She touched his face. "You shouldn't have worried."

"You have no idea. I drove like a bat out of hell to get here from Montana." He laid his head down on her stomach, cradling it with his hands. "Oh, God, I'm having four babies. I get light in the head sometimes thinking about it."

At least he wasn't mad that she hadn't told him that they were expecting. Suz felt a huge breath of relief escape her, too. "We're having twins. Where'd you get the idea we were having quads?"

He gazed up at her, his face a little haggard. And he seemed tired from the long drive, too. Suz resolved to get her husband into bed as soon as she could. "Daisy said we were."

Suz rolled her eyes. "You can't believe one thing Daisy Donovan says. If I didn't believe those stupid photos were real, why would you listen to anything that came out of her mouth?"

He gazed at her huge tummy with some alarm. "I believed her because Mackenzie had quads, and I distinctly recall you telling me that you were taking the same medication, some superbooster baby-maker stuff. I figured if your sister had done it, you'd feel right at home doing likewise." He took a deep breath. "But if there aren't four babies in there, Suz, we must be having a couple of basketballs."

"We're having twins." She smiled at him. "I hope you're not disappointed."

"Hardly." He kissed her stomach. "But when were you going to tell me?"

"Tomorrow. So you're right on schedule."

"Why tomorrow?" He raised a brow.

"Because the day after, I go in for a C-section, and I figured you'd want to be here."

"I wanted to be here for all of it!" He scowled. "And you knew I would darn well be here, so you didn't tell me!"

"Please don't be mad, Cisco. It's been crazy around here with Daisy and her father making everyone miserable." She took a deep breath. "We really disturbed a hornet's nest with our marriage, and then when it became obvious that I was pregnant, Daisy went a little crazy. Then when she learned I was having twins, she really seemed to realize that she was never going to get her way. Daisy not getting her way isn't pretty." Suz shrugged. "I've been working overtime trying to smooth things over. Judging by the photos Daisy sent around of the two of you, nothing's been smoothed at all."

"There isn't any Daisy and me," he growled. "I don't know what she sent, but I do appreciate you realizing it was a Daisy-plot."

"We all decided it was too convenient to be real."

"We? That sounds ominous. Who saw it?"

"All the usual suspects. Daisy sent the photos to everyone in her phone."

He lowered his forehead to her stomach. "I'm so glad you didn't fall for that nonsense."

"I've known Daisy almost all my life. I didn't lose a second's sleep."

"I don't believe that, but thank you for trying to comfort me." He looked up at her.

"It's the truth. Where is she, anyway? I figured she'd be hot on your heels."

"I think she gave up on me. The only reason she came to find me was to cause trouble. Those photos were a spur-of-the-moment lie when I fainted."

"You fainted! You weren't just asleep?"

He looked a bit embarrassed. "When she told me we were having quadruplets, I think my blood pressure freaked out."

"And you fainted!"

"Like an old woman who'd seen a ghost."

Suz laughed. "You poor thing. So where do you think our Crazy Daisy is?"

"I'm pretty sure she's in Montana." He kissed her hand, lingering long enough to give her shivers of pleasure. "Branch Winters doesn't take too kindly to trespassers. Once I learned you were pregnant—which I would rather not have learned from Daisy, by the way," he said, and she blushed. "I took off out of there instantly, as I mentioned. I called Branch from my truck to let him know there was a trespasser on his property. Just to slow her down a little, so she wouldn't follow me all the way home." He grinned, looking pretty pleased by that. "Last I saw Daisy, she was in custody."

"Custody!"

"Branch has a couple of teams of SEALs and other sorts of paramilitary types at his ranch. They help him out with a bunch of stuff, and he gives them a place to recharge, recoup, rewind." He shrugged. "Daisy's truck looked like it had been commandeered by them, and she was in the back of one of Branch's Jeeps being escorted to his ranch house, looked to me. Like I said, trespassing's not something he favors."

"They won't hurt her, will they?"

"Of course not! They'll just keep her from causing

trouble here for a few hours." He kissed her fingers. "So, I'm having sons, huh?"

"Actually, you'll be getting the chance to coach girls' soccer and lacrosse. We're having twin girls."

He let out a sigh of pure pleasure. "My world is turning pink. A wife and two little girls. I hope they look just like you."

She smiled. "I'm so very glad you're home."

He stood. "I'm going to grab some food. Can I get you anything?"

"You can tell me why you're walking so stiffly."

Her husband's eyes took on a cagey cast. "I drove straight here from Montana. I'm a little stiff from driving."

"We should probably make a pact from this moment forward that we always tell each other the truth. We don't have to protect each other as much as we have been."

He took a long look at her. "You're right. We're going to be parents. Parents should set good examples by being honest."

"Exactly. So, the injuries came from?"

"I may have had a small meeting with a bull that didn't go well."

Suz shook her head. "Didn't we talk about the fact that you're not the world's best bull rider, and I'm not the world's best swimmer? Let me see your ribs."

He raised his denim shirt, allowed her to walk her fingers along his torso, feeling for soreness. It was hard to focus on her task when there was a glory of muscle and dark skin under her fingers, but she forced herself to concentrate. "I'm calling the doctor for an appointment for you. And I'll wrap these ribs."

"I'm fine."

"No more fibbing. I remember a lot about this body, and I remember quite well that you don't wince when I touch you. Your ribs hurt."

"Like the devil," he confessed.

She smiled. "Bring me the special first aid kit I keep just for you. It has *Cisco* written on it."

"Hey!" he said, then shrugged. "Probably a good idea."

Suz watched her sexy man walk from the room, shifting a bit with discomfort. Everyone had tried as hard as they could to make her comfortable, but the past months had been long—especially without her husband.

It had been the right thing to do. She'd been shocked by the pictures Daisy had sent, though she wouldn't whisper a word of that to Cisco. Her phone had rung like mad from her friends, many of whom rushed over to comfort her in the face of Daisy's perfidy.

Darn Daisy, anyway. Suz hadn't needed comforting. She'd needed her husband.

Sam and Squint hurried into the room like eager puppies, heading straight to her sofa.

"We come bearing gifts!" Sam said.

"He says the same thing every time. It's like you're a one-trick pony, bud." Squint put down a bowl of chicken salad in which red grapes nestled, and a pitcher of a ruby liquid that looked an awful lot like sangria. "This is sangria," he said, setting down three glasses. "Miss Betty says it's pregnancy-appropriate sangria, which means it's some kind of organic crap—I mean, organic goodness. I think beet juice in seltzer water, with a splash of carrot and cucumber." He looked a bit woebegone. "Betty says that after you deliver the babies, she'll send over some almond-milk hot chocolate to celebrate. She's working on a new recipe."

Both men looked a bit concerned by the healthy twist to their diets. Suz laughed. "Thank you. This looks amazing."

"It's not real food, though." Sam dished out a plate of chicken salad for her, placing a few grapes beside it. "This is how she told me to serve this to you. And there's no bread because Miss Betty says she's being careful of food combining. Therefore, no grains with your meat." He sighed. "It's all hogwash to me, but whatever Betty says is law."

"Especially since her holistic approach appears to be working for you." Squint looked at her appreciatively. "You're looking good, Suz."

"Hey!" Cisco strolled in bearing a water pitcher and a platter of muffins. "What is all this?"

"This is us hitting on your girl while you're away," Sam informed him. He pounded Cisco on the back with enthusiasm, and then Squint took his turn.

"His ribs, fellows," Suz said, laughing. "I haven't wrapped them yet."

They stepped back quickly, and Cisco looked like he was trying to recover from the exuberant greetings.

"Again?" Squint asked. "You're hurt again?"

They shook their heads in disgust, sat down and snagged some grub.

"I'm not hurt," Cisco said. "I'm just a bit grazed."

"That means it's a three-wrapper," Sam whispered to Suz. "He'll require three layers of wrapping to get him back to scratch. He'll look like a mummy, but it's the only way to put our town Humpty Dumpty back together."

"You're terrible." Suz laughed, looking at Cisco, who seemed to weather his buddies' jibes with good humor.

"So, hitting on my girl, you said?" Cisco asked mildly.

"Just doing your job." Squint waved a muffin. "These are not Betty-approved for you, Suz. You have to wait thirty minutes after you eat to have one because I'm pretty sure this falls under the heading of grains. They sure are good, too. Zucchini?"

"I'm not sure." Cisco studied his. "I think mine's chocolate chip."

"And mine's gingerbread. I love gingerbread when it's cold outside." Sam slathered his with butter. "So you came home after Daisy rooted you out, huh?"

"Rooted me out?" Cisco raised a brow.

"You know. The photos." Sam waved his butter knife. "Those photos were some lulus, I can tell you. If ever there was a man to be caught with his pants down, I didn't think it would be you."

"Yeah. Caught with your hands in the cookie jar, too," Squint chimed in.

"With his nuts in the oven," Sam agreed.

"Buns afire," Squint added.

"I thought it was chestnuts roasting on an open fire?" Sam said. "Those photos sure gave new meaning to that holiday classic."

Cisco put his muffin down. "Maybe I should see these photos."

"No," Suz said. "They weren't that big of a deal. The guys are just teasing, aren't you?" She sent a warning look to both men. "And we've all deleted the photos, anyway. Haven't we?"

The men slowly nodded.

"Mine are gone," Squint said.

"Like the wind," Sam said.

"History." Squint looked from Suz to Cisco. "Zapped right into the dustbin of BC lore."

Cisco pushed his hat back. "I know when you two are lying, because you start talking real fast, which you're doing now. Hand over the phones so I can see the photos."

"Cisco," Suz said. "It's not important."

"Why are you hiding them?" He looked at her. "If it was no big deal, it won't matter if I see them."

Suz shrugged. "Okay. But you're not going to be happy."

"I'm already not happy." He accepted a phone from Sam, gazed at a couple of photos. His buddies stared at him, concerned, and Suz waited, her breath held.

"I'm going to kill her," Cisco muttered. He tossed the phone back to Sam. "At the very minimum, I'm going to file a law—"

"No, you're not," Suz interrupted. "You're not going to even acknowledge these photos."

"Why not?"

"Because it's what she wants. To cause trouble," Suz said. "We've talked about it—"

"Who's talked about it?"

"We have," Sam said. "We think if you cause trouble, it'll just make everything worse for everyone."

"How can it be worse when there are fairly naked photos of me being sent around the town with a fairly naked woman?" His voice blazed.

"Daisy's always been a troublemaker," Suz said quickly. "No one believed a thing they saw. Don't stir trouble, Cisco. We have our daughters to think of." Suz took a deep breath. "And what's even more important, I want you to call your friend Branch and tell him he has to call off his friends and let Daisy come home."

Chapter Ten

"Daisy's at Branch's?" Squint looked at him, surprised. "What's she doing there?"

"She stayed for an extra visit." Cisco didn't feel like talking about it. His blood still boiled over the photos. He was darn lucky he had such an understanding wife. Suz didn't seem to be near as bothered as he was by what Daisy had done. Maybe she'd grown a tough shell from all the years of Daisy's shenanigans—but he wanted to wring her neck. "Suz, Daisy's better at a distance, from my point of view."

"Cisco, it's got to end sometime. And for the sake of our children, I'd like it to end now. Please call Branch." Suz looked at Squint and Sam. "And I'd like you fellows to go escort her back home."

Their jaws dropped. "Us?" Sam said.

"As you know, Daisy and I aren't exactly on good terms," Squint said. "I tried my best, found greener pastures."

"Well, those greener pastures are no longer green, so it doesn't matter," Suz said.

Cisco perked up. "You quit seeing that woman from the town over?"

Squint looked a little embarrassed. "I was just trying to make Daisy a bit jealous. Thought it might make her take notice. But all she was ever interested in was you." He looked at Suz. "Don't make me go after her. Send Handsome Sam."

"I'll go," Cisco said, having no intention whatsoever of going but wanting to goose his brothers. "It should be me."

That shot Squint and Sam from their chairs. "We'll go," Sam said. "You have to be here for the birth of your daughters! Our namesakes!"

Cisco looked at his beautiful wife, who was more beautiful than ever, to his hungry eyes. "Their namesakes?"

Suz smiled at him, glowing. "If you approve."

"I *don't*."

They all laughed, but he didn't care to join in. "We're not naming our girls Handsome Samuelina and Squintina!"

They found that hilarious. "The names chosen so far are Samantha and Jennifer. Jennifer is as close to John as we could agree on, which represents John Lopez Squint Mathison, and Samantha is self-explanatory."

"All right, then," Cisco said gruffly. "You had me scared there for a moment."

They laughed at him again. Cisco sagged into the sofa. "This baby stuff is hard."

"Lightweight," Sam said, grinning.

"Weenie," Squint said, "we've done all the heavy lifting for you."

"Hey!" Suz exclaimed.

"Not that you're heavy," Squint said hurriedly. "We meant, we've done all your work for you, buddy."

"And I mean to talk to my wife about that, as soon as

you two hit the road." Cisco reached for another muffin and winked at Suz.

"I guess we'll go round up Daze." Squint got to his feet. "It's awkward, mighty awkward, going after a lady who wants nothing to do with me."

"Thanks, Squint." Suz smiled at her two messengers. "Tell her everything's forgiven back home."

"I don't think she cares." Sam grabbed the platter of muffins away from Cisco, slid them into a bag he commandeered from the kitchen. "Something for the road."

Cisco let his friends take off with the treats before turning to his wife. "So what's really going on?"

"What do you mean?"

She looked far too innocent. "Why are you sending Moe and Curly off to Montana?"

"Does that make you Larry?" Her gaze was teasing. "Of Three Stooges fame?"

"That was Ty. I'm my own man." He went to sit by his wife, leaning down to steal a kiss. A kiss he'd been wanting for far too long. She melted into him, her lips molding against his, and Cisco felt like he'd finally made it home.

"I wanted them to escort Daisy home to show there are no hard feelings from the Hanging H," Suz murmured against his mouth.

"And?" He waited to hear the rest of the plot. In BC, there were always many layers to even the simplest of plots.

"Maybe I'm trying to give Daisy a chance to see Squint in a hero's light. He'll show up to rescue her from evil Branch Winters and your mean prank you pulled. It really was mean," she said, kissing him again.

"Not mean enough, considering. Is that all?" Cisco

asked, knowing it all sounded too easy to be a BC plot. "Those are all very good points, but I have a sneaking suspicion there's more. Especially since I can practically discount point number two, as there'll be two conquering heroes who go to rescue the un-fair maiden. Daisy might just as well see Sam in the hero's light and fall for him, and then we'd have an even more miserable Squint on our hands."

"So you saw through his I'm-over-her story?"

"I did." He kissed her thoroughly, his whole soul alive with happiness.

"They're bringing Daisy back the long way," Suz admitted. "I want her gone long enough for me to give birth."

He considered his wife. "So peace and quiet can reign in Bridesmaids Creek?"

"Have you ever heard the fairy tale where the evil queen casts a spell over the baby princess because she wasn't invited to her birth party?"

"I wouldn't let Daisy near my daughters," Cisco said, his voice flat. "Don't worry."

"This is a small town. We all have to get along. But I'm giving birth while Daisy's not here to breathe bad karma on our big day."

He grinned. "You're cute when you're devious."

"It's not devious. It's practical." Suz leaned back to look at him. "But I don't want her stranded, and I don't want her being held at Branch's place." She smiled hugely, looking like an adorable pixie. "So I'm sending representatives to rescue her. Let bygones be bygones is my motto."

"Why can't Daddy Warbucks rescue her? Or her gang of five uglies?"

"She may have called any of the above. I don't know." Suz shrugged. "We'll know soon enough."

He glanced out at the gently falling dusk. A ranch truck rumbled down the drive, which meant his military brothers had departed. "I just don't know about sending Curly and Moe on such a delicate mission."

"They're SEALs. They'll handle it. I didn't want them here for the birth, either."

He perked up, recognizing for the first time that he'd been a little bit jealous of the time his buddies had gotten to spend with Suz during her pregnancy. "I should have thanked them for taking such good care of you. I was too jealous to man-up."

She laughed. "You were jealous of little ol' huge-as-a-house me being taken care of by your brothers, when I had to look at photos of you and Daisy in the altogether? Who's jealous here?"

He wasn't buying it. "You'd never be jealous of Daisy."

"I certainly didn't want her in a dental-floss thong near my husband." Suz giggled. "You looked like you were dead to the world. I actually felt sorry for you."

"Not nearly as sorry as I felt for myself." His insides cramped up. "Damn, Suz, when she told me you were having quadruplets, I'm pretty sure all the blood drained straight out of my head."

"Obviously." She laughed again. "You're going to have to make this right with Daisy eventually."

He bit the inside of his lip. "Pretty sure I can't. And I don't care to. In fact, I'd rather stick a hot flaming marshmallow in my eye than ever speak to her again."

Suz's fingers wound into his. "You'll feel differently when you hold your daughters for the first time. You'll want everyone to get along." She looked at him, her eyes huge. "After all the years my parents spent trying to fight off Robert Donovan, I'm determined to keep working on Daisy until she's given up every idea of taking our home. In fact, Daisy doesn't know it yet, but one day, she's going to think the Hawthorne girls are the closest things to real sisters that she's ever had."

That would take a miracle. Then again, who would have ever thought that Ty Spurlock would discover that he was Daisy's brother? Strange things happened in Bridesmaids Creek.

"Of course, I suppose this plan is contingent on how much guff Branch gave her for trespassing," Cisco said, more worried than he wanted to let on.

"You didn't really tell your friend that she was trespassing, did you?"

"I did," Cisco said. "I might have even told him that she was a stalker I couldn't get rid of."

His wife's mouth fell open. He didn't get a chance to explore it. "Cisco!"

"I'm sorry," he said. "All I could think about was the fact that my heart would break into a thousand pieces if she upset you. Hurt you in any way. Damn, Suz, she *is* a stalker. At least from my point of view." She'd kept him away from his wife for months. How would any normal red-blooded man feel about that?

Like he wanted Daisy kept nicely—comfortably—chained to a cactus in a faraway place for a year or two. He looked at his delicate, heavily pregnant wife. "I'll call him," he offered grudgingly.

"Thank you," she said, softening. "You're my hero."

And then she kissed him, and he totally felt like a hero. "I missed the hell out of you. I don't care what happens after this, I don't care what mayhem Daisy wreaks, I'm not leaving you again. The whole town can go bounce itself and Robert Donovan can groan all he likes, but I'm not spending one day without looking into your beautiful blue eyes, Suz Grant. Just so you know."

SAMANTHA AND JENNIFER made their way into the world, right as planned. Everything went smoothly, much to Cisco's vast pride. He was so proud of his wife he felt like his heart might pop any second. Just gazing at her as she cooed over her newborn daughters was enough to give Cisco a case of *love-struck* that wasn't ever going to go away. Every single day of their lives he knew he'd feel just like this: amazed by the petite, adorable woman who'd been brave enough to go against the BC grain to marry him.

"What do you think about your daughters?" Suz asked him.

"I think they look just like their mother, thankfully. And I see a lot of potential in them." He considered his daughters as the nurses tended them carefully. "Could be champion barrel racers, could teach high academics. The world is their oyster," he bragged, his heart swelling with love and pride in his daughters and beautiful wife.

It was more heaven than he deserved.

But hellfire blew into the room the next day. Daisy showed up in Suz's hospital room, bearing gifts. Or so she claimed.

"Daisy!" Suz exclaimed.

"Surprised to see me?" Daisy smirked. She was tall and her beautiful dark mane was wild and sexy—to Cisco it looked like she was just missing a broom to be any man's version of Bad Girl Finds Her Inner Sexy Witch.

She was the type of woman men would find spell-binding.

Cisco backed up a foot, peered at the shopping bag she carried with some approbation.

"I'm not exactly surprised to see you," Suz said, her tone a little annoyed. "But no one told me you were planning a visit today."

"Why wouldn't I want to take a look at Bridesmaids Creek's newest angels?"

Something slithered over Cisco's skin. Daisy had far too wild a look in her eyes for his liking. "Did Squint and Sam manage to catch up with you?"

"They did," Daisy cooed. "So did Branch Winters."

Uh-oh. He glanced at Suz, who shrugged at him. Clearly Daisy wasn't happy that he'd had her way-laid. Cisco shrugged. "Did you have a nice visit with Branch?"

"I did." She smiled at him. "Very nice. I think he may be in love with me."

Cisco took that in. "Branch?"

"Mmm." She sat in the only chair in the room, con-sidered him. "He's not the world's most sociable per-son, is he?"

"Maybe not." Cisco waited for Daisy's punch line—it was coming, he knew it was. "How does one go from trespasser and breaking and entering—into my room, by the way—to thinking that the ranch owner is your love slave?"

"Branch quickly realized that you weren't being en-tirely honest with him, after I explained that you had completely not recognized my truck."

"I see." He glanced at Suz, who shrugged. "Anyway, where are Squint and Sam?"

"They decided to stay a little longer at Branch's place. So I drove on back by myself. I was anxious to get home to Bridesmaids Creek." She smiled at Suz. "It's not every day we have a special delivery!"

Something was off but he just couldn't put his finger on what it was. Suz seemed in the dark, too. Daisy reached into her shopping bag, pulled out two identically wrapped white boxes with pink bows on top. "These are for your precious bundles of joy, Suz."

"Thank you, Daisy." Suz took the boxes, glanced at Cisco. This time the shrug came from him. Neither of them had any idea what was up Daisy's sleeve, so all they could do was paste on the polite smiles and hope for the best.

Suz unwrapped the first box, pulling out a beautiful glass bottle. Cuts in the bottle shimmered in the light, revealing what looked like water inside. "It's lovely, Daisy. What is it?"

"A crystal bottle filled with water from Bridesmaids Creek." Daisy smiled. "A keepsake. A memento of the magic that brought your little ones' parents together."

Something cold ran over Cisco's scalp, but as gifts went, it could actually be called thoughtful. Couldn't it? He couldn't judge by Suz's careful expression whether she was as unsettled as he felt.

She unwrapped the second beautiful box, holding up an identical lovely crystal bottle. This one was filled with dirt. Suz looked at Daisy. "I'm guessing dirt from Best Man's Fork?"

Daisy nodded happily. "A memento for your daughters! And now I must be off. I really just came back to BC to get my motorcycle."

"Where are you headed?" Cisco asked, not that he cared and not that he wanted to keep her from flying— er, leaving. But it seemed the courteous thing to ask, under the circumstances. And he was so perplexed by the gifts she'd given his daughters the question popped out before he could censor himself.

"Back to Montana." She grinned at Cisco, a temptress in one sizzling package and well aware of it. "I have a real yen to see those mountains from my bike."

Which meant Branch was under siege. But he was a big boy, he could handle himself. "Have fun. And thanks for the gifts."

"You're so very welcome." A smile that wasn't altogether open and charming crossed her face. "Best wishes to you both, and your new little angels."

She swept from the room. Suz looked at her husband. "Will you go get Cosette, Cisco? And bring her here as fast as you can?"

"Cosette? Why?"

Suz shook her head. "I can't tell you everything right now. But tell her it's urgent." She laid back, closing her eyes, and Cisco hurried off, aware that something was going on in BC that, as an outsider, he just couldn't understand.

But he understood that Suz was upset about something, so he made tracks.

COSETTE STARED AT the two beautiful bottles, as did Jane Chatham, whom Cosette had brought for backup. "This isn't good."

"No, it's not." Jane's eyes were huge and Suz felt sick.

"But the babies are so healthy." Cosette glanced at her friend. "Samantha and Jennifer came in at almost normal weight. The nurse said they won't be in the hospital long, and Suz can go home tomorrow most likely."

Cisco held Suz's hand, strong and warm fingers enveloping hers. "What does it mean?"

"We're not exactly sure." Cosette didn't take the stoppers off the bottles, Suz noticed. In fact, both Cosette and Jane seemed content to view them from six inches away, even though they peered at them closely. "Daisy would like you to think that these are gifts that say let bygones be bygones."

"But bygones are never gone," Jane added. "We saw the babies in the nursery, and they're not fussing or anything. Just resting happily, without a care in the world."

"What the hell is a bygone, anyway?" Cisco demanded.

"If you'd had any of Phillipe's tutoring sessions, you'd know it's of English derivation, circa the fourteenth century, meaning to forget past quarrels. That's a bygone," Cosette said. "It's very important to know your language history. We French are very aware of history." She pondered that for a minute. "Times like this I really miss Phillipe," she said on a sigh. "In fact, I miss him most of the time."

They all stared at her. Suz felt tears jump into her eyes. "Cosette! I'm so sorry!"

"No, no, I shouldn't have brought him up. The old donkey," she said, wiping her eyes as Jane handed her a lace handkerchief. "Talking about idioms and medieval history always makes me a little misty. He's so brilliant with all the dustier subjects, you know. My dusty little unmatchmaking husband. He just didn't have much business in this town, and spends too much time with his history tomes."

Their finances had to be in rough shape. They'd mostly relied on Cosette's income from the tea shop. Her matchmaking efforts were largely propaganda— though effective propaganda. "I'm going to empty these stupid bottles and put them up in the kitchen window where the sunlight can hit them," Suz said. "That'll kill all the germs and whatever may be lurking inside Daisy's scary gift."

"Scary?" Cisco looked at her. "Is dirt and water scary?"

"It is when it comes from Daisy. The outside of the gifts are elegant crystal, the inside is just plain weird." Suz shook her head. "I'm sorry. I shouldn't have dragged you down here, Cosette. I don't usually let superstitions unnerve me. Surely it's my raging hormones."

Robert Donovan walked in, his big frame over- whelming the room. "Hello, ladies, Cisco," he said, his voice booming.

Jane jumped to her feet. "What are you doing here, Robert?"

"I came to bring flowers to the new mother." He smiled, handing Suz a giant bouquet of beautiful lilies and roses. "And I sent two white rocking horses with the girls' names on them over to the Hanging H. Suz, I hope you'll accept these small tokens."

"Thank you," Suz said, not sure what else to say.

"Donovan," Cosette said, "I don't know that I trust this benevolent side of you. Aren't you trying to fore- close on the Hanging H and its business, the Haunted H?"

He nodded. "But that doesn't have anything to do

with welcoming two new members of Bridesmaids Creek society, does it?"

"It does," Cisco said. "I think Suz would rather you leave her alone than pretend to be a friend."

"Well, I can afford to be generous these days." Robert smiled. "I just put an offer on all the land where Bridesmaids Creek and Best Man's Fork are, and even as we speak, there are plans to put federal buildings there." He looked really pleased about that. "So all this worrying about luring folks to BC for a small-time haunted house won't be necessary anymore. Soon we'll have more people here than BC knows what to do with—which was the goal all along, right?"

Chapter Eleven

"Now what do we do?" Suz asked Cisco after Cosette and Jane departed, taking Daisy's gifts with them. The ladies had been completely shell-shocked by Robert's announcement, though they hadn't said much about that. They'd told Suz they would take care of emptying out the offending "offerings" of Daisy's gifts, and Cisco had been relieved.

His wife needed to have nothing on her mind except recuperating and bonding with their babies. "We love our new daughters. I really think I see the seeds of greatness in those girls," he said happily. "I'm anticipating them to be just like their mother."

"Peace Corps workers?" Suz teased.

"I'd be very proud." He sat on the hospital bed next to her. "Now rest. Don't think about anything. I'm going to take very good care of my wife."

Suz smiled at him, and his whole world lit up. "I love you, Cisco."

What man didn't want to hear that? Life just couldn't get any better than it was right now. Daisy was gone, off to bother Branch in Montana, obviously having given up on her dreams of seducing Cisco. Squint was going to be viscerally annoyed with him, but maybe love wasn't meant to happen between his buddy and the wild woman of Bridesmaids Creek. *Not my problem. Squint will have to suck it up.*

"Did Cosette and Jane seem like they were in a hurry to leave to you?"

Of course they'd been. Their brains had clearly gone into overdrive at the news Robert had delivered, which would entail plans being hatched. He shrugged. "They're always going ninety to nothing about something. But the only thing I plan on thinking about for the next twenty-one years is you and raising my daughters to be independent women like their mother. After that, I start Phase Two of our lives, which is keeping my shotgun rack full and primed for our daughters' suitors." He tried not to think about his daughters' one day being romanced by any Tom, Dick or Harry who decided to toss a heated glance their way. "I've got plenty on my plate without worrying about Cosette and Jane."

"Robert's announcement caught them totally by surprise. I don't see how he could have offered to buy treasured BC land without the town council's okay. Wasn't that part of the deal Jade struck with him? That he was never to do anything again without the council's permission, and nothing at all that wasn't beneficial to BC?"

Suz looked at him, searching for answers he didn't possess. "Why would he go back on their agreement? And clearly he has, because the gifts that Daisy gave the babies foreshadowed her father's announcement. She brought water from Bridesmaids Creek and dirt from Best Man's Fork, and called them mementoes. As if they weren't going to be here forever."

"This is true." Cisco got up, paced to the window. He, too, had been unpleasantly surprised by Robert's change of heart, especially as he knew Donovan spent plenty of time out at Jade and Ty's place with his granddaughters. They were the apples of his eye. "We don't have enough info to do anything right now. He made his announcement today for a reason, knowing we were too unsettled with new babies to make his life miserable."

"I can't wait to take our daughters home."

Cisco grinned. "I guess I'll go house shopping so I'll have a place to move my ladies to."

Suz looked at him. "What do you mean?"

"Can't raise a family in a bunkhouse."

"But I— Oh." She nodded. "Of course. I won't be living at the Hanging H anymore."

He sat on the bed next to her. "We're a family now. No more living apart."

"Yes." She smiled. "That makes even Robert's troubling news seem unimportant. Our first home!"

He nodded. "With us under one roof."

"It'll be very strange not to be living at the Hanging H. But I suppose if Robert has his way, it won't be the Hanging H much longer, anyway."

It wasn't a good thought. Cisco took Suz's hand in his. "Have any ideas where in town you'd like to live?"

"With you." Suz closed her eyes. "That's my dream come true."

He loved the sound of that. Cisco patted her hand. "Get some rest. I'll do a little asking around about available properties."

"As far away from the Donovan place as you can get us," she murmured.

Cisco pondered that as he got up to leave—and then it hit him: Robert Donovan was exactly the man with the right idea.

CISCO WAS WAYLAID by Cosette and Jane as soon as he walked through the doors of The Wedding Diner.

"Sit here, Cisco." Jane steered him to one of the white vinyl booths, which was far away from any diners who might overhear. "I'll get you a plate of something."

Cosette slid in across from him, her gaze directly on him. "There's a meat loaf special today."

"I'm not picky. I haven't had a good home-cooked meal in months." He frowned. "I can't remember when the last time was."

"You need a place of your own."

"Suz and I just talked about that very thing."

Jane brought back a plate of meat loaf, mashed potatoes and green beans large enough to feed a platoon, and three slices of coconut cake, which she put in front of each of them. A waitress followed her with three glasses of tea and three of water. Cisco grinned, delighted with steaming hot food. "This looks amazing. Nobody cooks like you do, Jane."

"I do," Cosette said, "but not meat loaf. No one can beat Jane's meat loaf. Now crepes and truffles, I can do. Although I'm getting out of practice with no husband."

Cisco hesitated in the act of forking up a huge, gravy-laden mouthful of fluffy potatoes. "How are you doing? And Phillipe?"

"We would be better had Robert Donovan never darkened the door of this town." Cosette shrugged. "But more to the point, we want to talk to you about his wild daughter."

"Daisy has given your daughters inappropriate gifts," Jane said. "Gifts that intend unhappiness."

"What?" He put his fork down. "Like a curse? I don't believe in curses."

"And you don't believe in Bridesmaids Creek shtick, either," Jane said. "Which is one of the reasons we're all in this boat we find ourselves rowing."

He put his fork down, studying his friends. "You're saying that everything that's happening in BC is my fault?"

"Isn't it?" Cosette's gaze stayed on him, and Cisco blew out the breath he'd been holding.

"You make a fair point, I suppose, as BC legend and lore goes." He shifted the Saint Michael medal at his neck under his shirt, the one that Squint had given him fresh out of BUD/S. The medal heated his skin. He moved it again, frowning, and dug into the meat loaf. "But it's not like talking to Donovan is going to do anything to take the heat off."

"No." Jane watched him tear into his meat loaf with a smile. He was too famished to eat more slowly, but neither of the ladies seemed to mind. They just watched him, waiting. Eventually, he put down his fork. "Not that I believe in that woowoo bit, but exactly how do you think Daisy put a curse on my daughters?"

"It was in the soil and the water of BC that she gave them. Which is why we took it," Cosette said. "We're not going to let anything happen to those precious bundles of joy of yours!"

"Look, this is all too Sleeping Beauty for me." Cisco had learned not to doubt everything in BC, but this was crossing a line, no matter how much he wanted to humor the darling elder ladies who'd always been so good to him. Maybe they were getting a bit on the loony side. Probably was understandable after a lifetime of living around questionable phenomena, which the Best Man's Fork run and the Bridesmaids Creek swim certainly were. "I'll talk to Squint and Sam to see if we can come up with any ideas of how to fix the land problem with Donovan. There has to be a way to stop his purchase of vast parcels of BC. Someone owned them for them to have been on the market. He just can't acquire town land that's not for sale."

"Donovan has friends in high places who see Bridesmaids Creek as the perfect place to plunk down their nefarious plots for a nuclear waste dump." Jane's eyes were huge.

"What?" Cisco couldn't have been more astonished if she'd said that a Ripley's Believe It or Not would be the next venture put into Bridesmaids Creek. "That can't be right."

"It's what we hear whispers of." Cosette looked completely distressed. "And where there are whispers, there are problems."

Cisco forbore to say that there were always whispers of one kind or another in BC. "I'll go find Squint and Sam right now, start working on a plan of some kind. We need to do something."

"Squint's gone again," Cosette said, and Jane nodded.

"Gone where?"

"After Daisy." Jane shrugged. "He's planning to waylay her on the road before she gets to Montana, tell her how he feels about her."

"That's a terrible idea." Cisco felt all hollowed out inside. "I wish he'd told me."

"He didn't want you to know. He knew you'd try to stop him," Jane said. "That's what he told Justin Morant."

"And Justin didn't try to talk sense into him?" Cisco

felt horrible for his buddy. Daisy was going to give him the smackdown of his life. What had gotten into Squint that had made him so head over heels for the wild brunette?

"There was no stopping him," Jane said. "In fact, he swore Justin to secrecy until he'd been gone six hours. That way, Squint knew he could make a clean getaway. And the only reason he told Justin is because—"

"Because Justin's boss man at the Hanging H," Cisco filled in. Well, Mackenzie and Suz were the real "bosses" but Justin did an excellent job overseeing the ranch and the hands. In fact, he'd pretty much single-handedly brought the Hanging H back from the disrepair it had fallen into.

"And Sam, well, you won't be able to talk to him very much, either," Jane said. "He's gone camping!"

"Camping?"

The ladies nodded. "He's gone into survival mode at Bridesmaids Creek. Says they'll have to blast him out of there before he'll let Donovan dam it up and drain it."

This was bad, really bad. His buddies had gone rogue without him. They wouldn't have come to him with their plans, not now, not while he and Suz had just had twins.

And as the ladies had so pertly pointed out, everything that was happening really could be laid at his door. Somehow he could have handled Daisy differently, let her down more gently. Not gotten caught up in the Bridesmaids Creek escapades. *Not participated in their silly lore in the first place.* "This is bad."

Cosette nodded. "It's definitely deeper cow chips than we normally find ourselves in."

"And we're such a peaceful, quiet town," Jane said, and Cisco didn't detect any irony in her tone. "I'd give anything to go back to the days where we used to wish for a little excitement!"

Cisco stood. "I'd better head back to Suz. I didn't mean to leave her alone this long."

"I'll wrap up your food. And I'll send an extra meal over for Suz. What a homecoming we're planning for her and the girls!" Jane said, getting up to make a to-go basket.

Once the basket was put into his hands, Cisco kissed the ladies on their cheeks and headed off.

He and his wife had a lot of things to discuss.

"How do you feel?" Cisco looked at his wife with some surprise, as she tried to cross the room. "Should you be doing that? You look like you're in pain."

"I am in pain. And yes, I should be doing this. I want to go down and see the girls in the nursery. It doesn't feel right to carry those babies for so long and not have them right here with me."

That was part of what worried him. Suz wasn't going to want to take time to rest, not when she wanted to spend every moment with their girls. He debated for a moment not telling her the news he'd learned at The Wedding Diner—realized what a terrible mistake that would be if Suz learned it from someone else. They'd discussed being totally honest with each other, hadn't they?

"It's going to work out. By Christmas, we'll all be together." A smile lit her face, and Cisco felt like he'd helped his wife a little.

She moved back toward the bed, sinking down into it. "I'll be ready to go home. Well, to the Hanging H. Then we can start looking for a house."

"Speaking of looking for homes, we may have to stay at the Hanging H for a while." Cisco pulled a chair up next to her bed. "Squint and Sam have taken off."

"Taken off?"

"To various destinations." For now he wanted to gloss over the Daisy angle. He was still reeling over the notion that all the recent bad luck in BC could be parked at his door.

"Without saying goodbye? Without seeing the babies?" Suz was surprised. "That's not like them!"

He rubbed his chin, wondering how much to tell her. "You've heard of Yosemite Sam? We have our own Bridesmaids Creek Sam right here. Sam's staked out the creek to keep Donovan from damming it up and pouring concrete over it."

"Concrete!"

"There's a thought process that Donovan's scooped up all our favorite haunts and they'll soon be nuclear waste sites."

Suz started laughing. "That'll never happen."

He perked up. "No?"

"No. You underestimate the good people of this town." She smiled at him. "Come sit by me. And then I'll let you leave and release the knight from his bondage."

"Sam? Bondage?"

"Well, you remember that Daisy's gang tied Squint to a tree. Stands to reason that Sam might think of something equally dramatic. Lashing himself to a tree to thwart Donovan's bulldozers."

"It's not a bad idea." He sat next to his wife on the bed, longing to hold her. "If you want to give me some more comforting words, you can tell me that it's totally laughable that Squint has gone after Daisy."

"That's more serious." Suz considered that for a minute. "Can't you stop him?"

Cisco was surprised. "Why would I want to?"

"A woman doesn't want a man who chases her, when she's already turned him down." Suz looked sad for Squint.

"I could catch him, I suppose. But then he'd be mad at me, and frankly, I've already got the rest of the town sort of annoyed with me."

"Who?" Suz frowned. "No one should be annoyed with you!"

"There's a theory that I didn't play by the rules, and therefore we find ourselves in deep Donovan doo."

"That's silly."

"It's BC."

"Don't think about it," Suz said. "Go unlash Sam from his post, for heaven's sake. Tell him we appreciate the manly effort, though. We really do." She thought for a moment. "He'd make such a nice prince, if he was of a mind to be one."

There was no point in discussing that angle. Suz seemed certain that Sam wasn't interested in the altar, and one thing Cisco had learned was that he could trust his wife's intuition. "Squint's cruising for a bruising."

"You can't feel responsible for him. He's convinced Daisy's the one. She's convinced he's not." She wrapped her fingers through his. "That story could have been ours."

"No, it couldn't have. You are not Daisy."

"What if you'd fallen for her?"

He shuddered a little. "Well, none of this would

be happening. Life would go on, happy and blowing unicorn-shaped bubbles in the land that time forgot."

Suz giggled. "Poor Daisy."

"If I was their only game plan, they made a mistake not having a backup plan." Cisco kissed his darling wife, lingering over her lips for a moment. "I guess I'll go let Yosemite Sam know he can leave his post."

She smiled. "Thank you for bringing me dinner."

"Tomorrow, I take you home. Our first real day together as husband and wife, and parents, under one roof."

"Well, along with Mackenzie and Justin and their four babies. But you're handling this awfully well."

"I am, aren't I?" He winked. "Good night, beautiful."

"Good night."

He left her dinner close by for when she was ready to eat. He strolled to the nursery to take a peek at his daughters, who were snuggled up like pink-wrapped, pink-topped angels. He was a father. Those were his daughters. Cisco felt himself swell with pride.

Life didn't get better than this.

LIFE WAS DEFINITELY stranger than fiction, and Cisco realized he was looking at the strangest slice of life yet when he found Sam at the creek, with a guitar and a basket of food, singing along with Daisy's gang at the top of their lungs.

From a musical point of view, it was pretty hard on the ears. Cisco winced and sat down on the Native American blanket next to his friend, eyeing Daisy's gang of five rowdies with some approbation. "Brother, that's not pretty. You're gonna kill wildlife. Owls and bats and things with sensitive hearing. Or forever damage them psychically with your caterwauling."

Sam twanged one last riff and put his guitar down. "There's no one to hear but us."

"Yeah, but even your shadow's in pain. You never told me you were such a bad singer." He couldn't figure out why Daisy's gang was suddenly the equivalent of an off-key band with his friend, but a couple of bottles lying around gave him an idea.

"I'm pretty sure you knew I wasn't a pop star in Afghanistan."

Yeah, but they'd all been hard-pressed to carry a tune over there, and no one had cared, anyway. "I just thought you wailed like a girl for grins."

"I was just warming up. If you'd arrived thirty minutes later, the rough spots would have been out of my voice."

Cisco doubted that. "So, listen, I hear you're down here to save the town, buddy."

Sam looked at him. "Just trying to make a statement."

Cisco nodded. "You've made it. Let's head back to the ranch before you do yourself a mischief." Or Daisy's gang did him a mischief. Cisco didn't like any part of this setup.

"Mischief is all right with me."

Cisco eyed the local group of bad news. "Carson, Dig, Clint, Red, Gabriel. What's happening in your tiny-brained slice of the world?"

The men grunted greetings in return.

"We thought we'd hang out a little now that Daisy's gone," Sam explained.

Cisco could think of very little news he'd like less

than this. "You fellows looking for a new ringleader? Can't operate on your own?"

"We like Sam," Carson said. "He doesn't have his head up his butt."

"Well, that's debatable." Cisco decided to try to get some answers out of them. "Couldn't you stop Daisy from escaping your clutches?"

Dig shrugged. "We're just branching out our friendships, Cisco. Connections are important. Relax."

"I could relax," Cisco said dryly, "if you hadn't tied Squint to a tree to keep him from winning not that long ago."

"That was your fault." Clint glared at him. "Madame Matchmaker said you would pay us to slow your buddy down. So far we haven't seen a bit of green."

Cisco counted to ten, wondering once again at the white-gloved perfidy of one of the sweetest women he'd ever had the pleasure of pitting wits against. "Why in the world would I have wanted Squint slowed down?"

"So you could win Daisy." Red Holmes looked at him in disgust. "But then you dishonored her by not marrying her. Dude, that is not the way things are done in this town. If you're going to live here, you have to honor the creed."

"Yeah, Cisco, honor the creed," Sam said, laughing. He pushed his hat back on his head to study Cisco, his brown eyes laughing, and Cisco wanted to grab his hat and make him eat it.

"We ought to pound you for what you did to Daisy," Gabriel Conyers said. "She's a nice girl. What you did was wrong."

"Here's the thing. I couldn't like a woman who my buddy likes, could I? That's not honorable, is it?"

They appeared to take that in.

"If Squint was meant to be with her, he would have won," Carson pointed out. "At least one of the races, anyway. He came up short. No woman's going to want a man who can't make the grade."

"He came up short," Cisco said patiently, "in one of the races because you fellows tied him to a tree."

"Again," Dig said, just as patiently, "because we were commissioned to do so by Cosette."

There was no reason to further interrupt the guitar-playing, moon-howling miscreants. Cisco eyed his buddy with disgust. "You haven't even been by to see the babies."

"No, but I do congratulate you on your pink-ribboned success." Sam grinned at him. "All our buddies have had girls. Which ratchets up Bridesmaids Creek's issue, I'd say. All ladies, no gents. The fairy tale lives on. Or horror story, from the ladies' point of view."

"You know, you could find a woman and see if you could do any better," Cisco said.

"Not me." Sam stretched his boots out, eyed the scuffed toes with satisfaction. "I've done my duty by my country. For the rest of my life, I'm only doing duty for myself."

Cisco shook his head. "Why are you down here again?"

"To enjoy the peace and quiet."

"To chain ourselves to trees or rocks to keep Donovan from bulldozing this place," Dig said. "We're human shields."

"This isn't going to work. We need a better plan," Cisco said.

"You got one?" Gabriel asked.

"I've barely slept since my children were born," Cisco admitted. "But surely between us, we should be able to think of a winning plan."

"So you want our help," Carson said flatly.

"Uh, sure. Yeah." *Team building sucks, especially with the lack of qualified teammates, but it'll have to do.*

"If we're going to help get you out of the mess you created," Carson said, and Cisco had to bite his lip, "you're going to have to take Bridesmaids Creek more seriously than you have."

"Yeah, man, not just take off with one of our best girls," Dig said, glaring.

"And break the heart of one of our other best girls," Red said. "Not cool, man. Wasn't cool at all."

Cisco wondered if he was ever going to get out of the alternative universe he appeared to have fallen into. "So do you have any suggestions?"

"We do." Sam nodded, setting his guitar down. "We think—the fellows and I—believe you're going to have to speak to Monsieur Unmatchmaker."

"Phillipe?" Cisco wondered what had gotten into his best buddy, a man who'd fought beside him in Afghanistan, whom he knew as well as anyone. At this moment, he hardly recognized the Sam who was clearly plotting with the enemy. "What does Phillipe have to do with anything?"

"Monsieur Unmatchmaker undoes what his wife does," Dig explained. "Cosette's good, but on occasion, she misfires big-time. She did with you."

"And Mackenzie," Gabriel reminded them. "It could be possible that the Hawthorne sisters are resistant to Cosette's brand of magical assistance."

Cisco stared at the group of six village idiots, of

which Handsome Sam clearly had a brand-new membership card. "Or maybe all this BC nonsense is just nonsense. Cosette doesn't have a degree in matchmaking, and Phillipe is just a husband who's trying to figure out a way to take care of his wife. Ex-wife, now, I guess," he said, feeling miserable for Phillipe.

"You have to learn to appreciate the ways," Red said darkly.

The ways of BC. *This is just not going well.* "Is that why you five are single? Because you appreciate the ways of BC so well?"

"Not cool." Clint Shanahan finally spoke up, after listening to all the back and forth silently for ten minutes. "We're single because we haven't been ready to give up the life of BC bodyguards."

"Bodyguards?" Cisco glanced at Sam, who shrugged.

"Protectors. We protect BC from bad stuff. Notice we have no crime here," Dig said.

"I thought you were the criminal element," Cisco said, "not to be too obvious for you or anything."

They stared at him, dismayed.

"Hey, your friend really is a pain," Carson told Sam.

"He can be at times," Sam agreed.

"So if I go see Phillipe, won't he unmake my marriage? If one believes in conventional wisdom, isn't that exactly the point of what he does?"

He received five nods from Daisy's gang. Maybe Sam's gang now. Cisco shook his head. "I don't know what's in those bottles you fellows are drinking—"

"This is homegrown," Sam said, proud as a new mother, "made by Phillipe himself. But don't tell anyone."

Cisco looked at the pile of bottles around the men,

who'd clearly been having quite a picnic under the stars. "It doesn't look like it's much of a secret. And anyway, if you think I'm going to let anyone tinker with my marriage, you're dead wrong." It was the dumbest thing he'd ever heard of. "But I will run by and check on Phillipe, because I haven't had a chance to see him since he and Cosette moved out of their shops."

They nodded their approval.

"And you," Cisco said to Sam, "you're hanging out with a bad element."

"Hey!" Clint exclaimed. "Who's to say you're not the bad element? You're the one who's caused all the trouble in BC! Everything was fine until you came along!"

Cisco looked at Sam for backup. His erstwhile buddy, whose back he'd had many a time in bad places, merely shrugged. "You know, SEALs stick together."

Sam nodded. "It's true. Have a beer. Join us. You need to loosen up a bit."

Cisco shook his head and departed. Matters were getting so weird around BC he wasn't certain they could ever be fixed. The good news was that his marriage was solid, in spite of the wacky ways of the small town.

He'd make a quick check-in on Monsieur Unmatchmaker, cheer the poor guy up, then head back to the hospital to see his babies and kiss his darling wife. Then he had to get on a serious house-hunt for his family.

His rodeo days seemed far away—which was probably a good thing. "I'm going to put my little girls in swimming lessons and rodeo lessons as soon as they can walk," he vowed, banging on the front door of Phillipe's tiny new abode. The little wood frame house was as far from Cosette's as it could be, and lacked the charm of their old place. Cisco's heart weighed heavy inside him—but there wasn't much he could do to help. He was no expert on marriage, after all. Cosette and Phillipe were—but look what had happened.

Best he stick to the script of Chief Comforter.

Then he could tell Sam and his new gang to blow their whole it's-your-fault-because-you-disrespected-the-BC-ways out of their collective hats.

Phillipe opened the door. *"Bonjour!"* he exclaimed. "Please come in! This must be my day for visitors!"

The fragrance of incense hit Cisco the second he walked into the small house. Colorful strands of beads hung in a doorway, separating the hallway from the den. Cisco followed Phillipe into the small room, where colorful cushions lay on the floor. Not a stick of furniture was to be seen.

"So this is your new place," Cisco said, wondering why it looked like a time capsule from the sixties had been deployed in the room. He half expected to see a hookah on the floor. Instead of a hookah, Robert Donovan took up one of the colorful soft cushions, his boots crossed in front of him in a relaxed yoga-type pose. Cisco winced.

"Donovan," he said by way of abbreviated greeting, "what the hell are you doing here?"

Chapter Twelve

"I might ask you the same," Robert shot back. "Anyway, take a seat and relax. That's what we do here."

Cisco didn't know if he could relax with Robert on the premises. He glanced at Phillipe. "You do this often?"

"All the time. It's good for your mental state. I also give lessons."

"I had no idea you were a yogi." Cisco took a cushion as far from Donovan as possible.

"Working on my journey," Phillipe said. "And I presume you wouldn't be here if you weren't in great need of working on yours."

"I don't need to—" Cisco began, belatedly remembering he was here on a mission of—oh, hell, he didn't know why he was here. Whatever the plan was had been shot all to hell. He gave Donovan the side eye and pulled off his boots. "Yeah, I'm here to work on my journey. And I'm hoping you can help."

"Breathe deeply," Phillipe intoned, sitting down on the floor. They now formed a rather unfriendly triangle of sorts. Cisco wasn't sure he could close his eyes and concentrate on relaxing when his enemy was across from him. "In with the good air, out with the bad."

Cisco wondered how fast he could duck out of the session of finding himself without hurting Phillipe's feelings. After all, he'd come here to comfort him, hadn't he?

With his eyes closed and something like hippie music suddenly playing softly in the background, draining him of his desire to argue or pluck anybody's harp strings, he belatedly remembered his mission was to see Phillipe in the capacity of Unmatchmaker.

Whatever an unmatchmaker had to offer him, he couldn't have said at this strangely starting-to-relax moment.

"Breathe," Phillipe said, and Cisco tried to.

"Feel your cares just fall away," Phillipe said, and Cisco's eyes snapped open.

"My cares can't fall away, Phillipe," he said, "because Donovan is sitting on the cushion across from me like a mushroom that's been growing in the dark too long."

"Hey!" Robert glared at him. "No talking in the circle!"

"The circle, my foot—" Cisco began, and Phillipe said, "Breathe, fellows. Discussions can wait until after we're in touch with our inner guides—"

"I'm in touch with mine," Cisco said. "And my inner guide is telling me that someone needs to explain to Mr. Donovan that he just can't go digging up half of Bridesmaids Creek to sell to whomever for a nuclear waste facility!" Cisco jumped to his feet. "And what the hell are you doing, Phillipe? You're a lot of things but you are not a hippie, my friend. Did they even have hippies in France?"

Phillipe appeared chagrined, his inner guide good

and rattled. He turned off the music, flipped on a light floating in a small incandescent bowl and looked at Cisco. "Cisco, you have to calm down. The path forward is through forgiveness."

Robert hopped to his feet, too. "I'll forgive him when he does the right thing by my daughter!"

"The right thing?" Cisco was stunned. "What right thing?"

"You were never honest with Daisy," Robert pointed out. "You let her waste her chances on you, when you were already married!"

"As uncomfortable as I am to admit that you're right, you're right, Donovan," Cisco said. "Phillipe, how do I make things right? For Daisy? And for all of Bridesmaids Creek?"

"My suggestion is that the two of you let bygones be bygones, first of all," Phillipe said to Cisco and Robert, his tone a bit stern.

"And you can go rescue my daughter from this friend of yours in Montana! This is all your fault," Robert fumed.

"Daisy's a grown woman," Cisco said. "I doubt I have to rescue her from anyone."

"Be that as it may, I want my daughter here, not in Montana. That's my only daughter." He considered that for a moment. "Ty's not here, either, so I have no family of my own around," Robert said, his voice trailing off. "And I'm sure that you can appreciate that Daisy is the apple of my eye."

"I'm very well aware that Daisy is a daddy's girl." Cisco took a deep breath. "Robert, I can't change the fact that she's gone off. She's a grown woman, and not too different from her old man."

Robert glowered. "I'm sure there's an insult in there."

"Perhaps there could have been one, but not this time." Cisco sat back down on a soft cushion on the floor, feeling like diplomacy would win the day. "Squint's gone after her, if it's any consolation."

"The problem is, son, and what you don't understand, is that private investigators aren't that expensive to hire." Donovan shifted onto a cushion, staring warily across at him.

"What does that mean?" Cisco watched as Phillipe headed off to check his incense sticks and root around in the kitchenette off the small den.

"It means I know who you are, and I know who John Squint Mathison is. And so does Daisy. She's not going to be interested in your buddy Squint."

Cisco went very still. "What exactly do you mean?"

Phillipe came back in with three shot glasses and a bottle of whiskey. "Just to take the edge off our visit." He sat down, poured some shots. "At least it's not paper cups, huh? Cosette wanted all the crystal and china kind of stuff, and it didn't go with my more earthy décor, anyway."

Cisco hesitated before he eviscerated Donovan for being a no-good sneaky snake. "I'm sorry as hell, Phillipe. I should have told you how sorry I am about you and Cosette. Which can be laid squarely at your door, Donovan. If you hadn't messed around with their finances, and pulled their shops from underneath them, they'd probably still be married. Why are you here for yoga lessons, anyway?"

"Phillipe invited me." Donovan shrugged. "He said Cosette had noted that I might have a little blockage in my carotid, so I went and had that checked. Turned out she was right. Now I'm on some thinners and feel great." He glanced at Phillipe. "I don't know how she knew."

"Oh, Cosette knows things." Phillipe raised his glass. "Here's to happiness in BC."

"I'm not drinking to that," Cisco said, "until Donovan tells me exactly what he thinks he knows about my life." Even he and Suz had never talked about his family. He sure didn't want Donovan digging around like a nosy badger. It was a sore spot, something he'd tried to get away from for a long time.

But Daisy's obsession with him would make more sense.

"So it turns out that John Mathison is the son of gypsies, really. Small-time clowns and barrelmen, from his grandfather to his father. His mom did some cowboy preaching. They followed the rodeo from town to town in a beat-up trailer. Raised three children that way. Mathison went into the SEALs to make a better life for himself."

Cisco's eyes narrowed. "And his country, as did we all."

"Not so much for your side of the story," Donovan said. "You fared a little better. Your mother, Chloe, and your father, Fernando, had four children—Damien, Mateo, Jean-Michel and you. In fact, you're the black sheep, aren't you?"

Cisco got to his feet, set his shot glass on a side table, untouched. "I'm going."

"I didn't know you had all this family," Phillipe said, looking up at him. "We're a very family sort of town. Maybe you should bring your brothers here! We could introduce one of them to Daisy!" He snapped his fingers, inspired. "In fact, that may be the missing key! Cosette said there was some missing key that links you and Squint together, and that's why Daisy's been so confused. Cosette says there's been a transfer of energy keeping her fixated on you, but the real man of her heart is someone else. One of your brothers is probably that someone, and Daisy's picking up the wrong signals. She has crossed wires or something." He looked triumphant. "I don't know how Cosette knows these things, but she always does. She always said you weren't the man for Daisy."

"I think everyone in the town knows that," Robert growled. "And I'm certain as anything that a small-town gypsy isn't the man for my daughter. She'll never fall for Squint."

Cisco backed up. "I'm not bringing my brothers here, so if that's what you're both angling for, forget it."

"Royalty's royalty," Donovan said, "even if they make special brownies and chocolates for a living."

"What?" Phillipe said, and Cisco said, "Mind your own business, Donovan. Mind your own damn business."

He went out, got in his truck. Headed to the hospital, proud of himself for not punching Donovan in the nose.

"I DON'T UNDERSTAND," Suz said, staring at her husband. She was set to leave the hospital tomorrow, her babies were starting to really thrive and Christmas wasn't that far off. It had seemed to her that her world was suddenly a very bright place. "What do you mean, Robert Donovan had you investigated?"

"He's a sly dog, I'll give him that. But the fact remains, I should have told you everything. And I hope that you will listen to me, let me tell you what I didn't mention to you in the beginning."

"I'm listening," Suz said, her whole body turning cold.

"It's complicated," he said, "but my family owns a few things."

Suz waited. "Is it an uncomfortable topic for you?"

"I just don't go home all that often. Never, actually," he said. "It's been said I've got restless leg."

"The medical syndrome?" Suz asked. "Something you should see a doctor for?"

"No, the kind of restless leg that causes me to see a travel agent for. Or the military, which I did. And then rodeo." He nodded, pretty happy to have found a way to put that into words. "I'm the oldest child. I didn't want to do the family thing. My brothers are much more like the old man than I'll ever be."

"A black sheep of sorts."

"That's what Robert called me." He shrugged. "Mom's family claims roots from some sort of French royalty. Hence the Olivier. Dad's family claims some sort of Spanish royalty, or lineage of high something or other, hence the Francisco Rodriguez bit." He pondered that for a moment. "Actually, they may have split the deck on Francisco. That one might go either way."

"Royalty?" Suz looked puzzled.

"Well, not in the sense where one runs around wearing a crown and whatnot. And it's all very distant. But they own a winery in France, and some stuff in Spain. Have a place in Virginia that's pretty nice, but not for me. The brothers run all that stuff. There's a lot to do, and I really should feel guilty about not helping with the family business, but I don't." He was ready to change the subject. "I guess I should mention that one of the brothers actually makes and sells artisan cheeses and chocolates, and I'm not so certain that he hasn't branched into special brownies."

"Special brownies?"

"Yeah. The kind that seems very popular with the peace-and-love crowd. But I can't swear by that. It's just something I heard whispered about once in the family. I think I was the black sheep until that business venture kicked off about ten years ago. Then I think Dad decided maybe he had bigger worries than the fact that I wanted to go into the navy."

"Are you saying our girls are descended from some kind of royalty?" Suz asked, her adorable face looking quite worried. "I'm not exactly going to fit in with that kind of crowd."

"You and me both." He shook his head. "It's okay. We only have to go home about once every ten years or so. Everybody's happier that way." He was just glad she was here with him. "I sent them a photo of you around the first time I ever met you. You were the most darling spitfire, and I knew the moment I met you that you were going to be someone special in my life."

"You sent a photo of me when you first met me?"

"Around that time."

"When I still had blue hair and piercings?"

He winked. "The family said you looked like a very intelligent sort. That's high praise in my family. Anyway, I hope you didn't change on my behalf. The Suz I met was the one who took my breath away."

Suz stared at him. "You're a navy SEAL. That's the man I married. You're a great swimmer, and not so good a bull rider. Where did the rest of this story come from? Is this because you didn't marry Daisy?"

Cisco sat across from her, his eyes dark. He looked haunted. Suz tried desperately to understand why he'd be telling her this now. They'd never talked about his family before, not to any great extent—but she knew they were from Virginia. And that he'd had what he'd called restless leg—the type of condition that had made him go into the navy, and then follow the rodeo.

But that restless leg seemed to have gotten a lot less restless now that he was married and a father. Or at least Suz felt it had.

"Donovan also dug up the fact that Squint's family isn't royalty." Cisco shook his head. "Donovan seems to think Daisy knew all this."

"And she preferred you."

He shrugged. Obviously Daisy would be after a royal title—no matter how minor. Suz had to admit her feelings felt a wee bit bruised that Cisco hadn't told her. "I wish I'd known before Daisy and her father did."

"Me, too." He looked grim. "I wasn't keeping anything from you, Suz. Honestly, I haven't been home in nearly ten years. I *am* the black sheep, and I don't care. Once our daughters were born, it popped into my mind one day that, eventually, they'd have to meet their grandparents. It isn't a scenario that really makes me happy. So I ignored it. I'm just not close to my family, and I consider you and the girls my family. That's it."

Suz couldn't imagine not being close to her family. Mackenzie had been her best friend and support for so many years—all her life. And they'd been very close to their parents, were still trying to keep their memory alive by running the Hanging H ranch and the Haunted

H. "I guess Mr. Donovan is very happy he found all this out about you. Anything to cause a problem between us."

"I hope it doesn't."

Suz didn't want to admit that her feelings were hurt. Yet nothing Cisco had told her changed anything in their lives: they were still married, and he wasn't close to his family.

It just didn't matter.

"I'm glad I didn't have to hear it from them." Suz waved her husband to come sit by her on the bed, and when he did, she put her head against his shoulder. "I love you so much. Nothing is ever going to come between us."

"They'll try," Cisco said, his voice a little defeated. It was the first time she'd ever heard him sound that way. "But hang with me, Suz. I swear you'll never regret it."

She closed her eyes.

The Donovans could have their regrets and their vendettas.

I'm going to keep my family together.

Chapter Thirteen

A thousand thoughts flew through Suz's mind. She sat up straight suddenly, joggling her husband, who took that as an invitation to hold her in his big, strong arms.

Which felt wonderful—if she wasn't so worried about the past coming between them. Her husband hadn't shared all of the dark shadows in his life before her, and she'd married him without knowing that much about him. "If Daisy's so bent on being married to a title, why has she gone after Branch?"

"Phillipe's theory is that she thinks I may come after her."

Suz hesitated. "Why?"

"Because she's going to Branch, who is my friend."

She wrinkled her nose. "Like a Prince Charming rescuer sort of situation?"

"I guess. Truthfully, I couldn't fathom the way Donovan and his daughter think, even if I'd lived in BC for ten years."

He tucked her closer to him, and Suz snuggled up tight. Inhaled him. Dreamed of the day they could make love again. "You're going to have to go after her," Suz said.

"No. Absolutely not." Cisco leaned away so he could

look down at her. "I'd gnaw off my own foot first. Both feet. Besides which, I'm sure Squint has it all under control."

They were silent for a moment. "I don't think you believe every word of that."

"I know that I'm not leaving my wife and brand-new daughters to go chasing after a woman who has tried her best to destroy my marriage."

"I don't believe in my heart that's what Daisy wants. I've been thinking about this. Now that I know that your attraction is a very minor title and not these big, strong muscles—" she teased.

"It might be the muscles," Cisco said.

"But it's likely more that she has visions of tiaras dancing in her head."

"True. Knowing Daisy, it's a fair possibility."

"So take me and our daughters home to the Hanging H. Then you go after Daisy."

"I suppose it goes without saying that I'm going to do whatever you want me to do, eventually," he said, and she curled her fingers into his.

"I think you should go after them, and drag Squint away. Then Daisy will have to think twice about what she's giving up."

"Is that how the female mind works?"

"Maybe," Suz admitted. "We can be a bit slow at times."

"So can guys. That being said, I'm making a judgment call here. I'm not going."

"If you don't, Daisy's going to get to Montana with Squint hot on her trail."

"Which you think will make him less appealing."

"Probably. Daisy doesn't want what she can have. If

you'd known her for as many years as I have—since she first came to BC as a little girl—you would know it's just the way she is."

"Probably most women," he mused.

"I knew I wanted you from the first moment you said you wanted me," Suz said. "In fact, I wanted your baby."

He perked up visibly. "That was awesome. You scared me a little, but it was awesome." He kissed her lips gently. "Thank you for understanding why I hadn't gotten around to sharing about my family. It's just something I try hard not to think about."

"I should have told you I was pregnant," Suz said softly. "Hearing it from Daisy wasn't the way I wanted you to know. We've both kind of erred that way."

They sat silently for a moment, then Cisco got up. "There's got to be a way to get Donovan not to carve up Bridesmaids Creek."

"The only thing I know of that changes a man's heart is a woman," Suz teased.

"We're in short supply of women that will date him." Cisco paced, turned to look at her. "Despite the abundance of ladies we have in BC, none of them will go out with him."

"That's a shame. I really feel like there's a good man in there. Somewhere."

"Even his wife wasn't too keen on him, according to Ty Spurlock."

Suz shook her head. "I'd like to think people can change."

"Maybe. Maybe not."

"Tomorrow, when I go home, I'm going to get the tree put up. And start planning the happiest Christmas of our lives." Suz smiled at her big, sexy husband. "I guess I don't want to think about the Donovans anymore."

"Yeah." He nodded, his face finally relaxing into a bit of a smile. "Our last night to sleep in the hospital."

"You didn't have to stay with me. But it meant a lot that you did," Suz said. "At least we can see our babies together."

"I wouldn't have missed it for the world," Cisco said. "Being a father and a husband is an even better ride than rodeo."

Suz laughed. "As I recall, rodeo wasn't your strong suit. You're going to be a much better husband and dad than bull rider."

"That's the plan."

Suz closed her eyes, letting contentment wash over her.

"Did I tell you that Sam's hanging out with Daisy's gang now?"

"Why?" She found that hard to believe. "Why would Sam want to do that?"

"I don't know what he's up to. Definitely something, I just don't know what. But Sam's always working an angle." He sat back down next to her, and she made room for him in the narrow bed. "And even more disturbing, Phillipe has gone hipster."

Suz giggled. "What does that mean?"

"Beads, vibes, yoga, the whole thing. And as weird as it sounds, it actually wasn't that bad. I kind of liked it. His place is real small, though."

Suz shook her head. "I believe in my heart that if we could get Cosette and Phillipe back together, everything that's amiss in BC would fall into place."

He sat up. "Had they ever talked about divorce before?"

"They always bickered. In a loving sort of way. But Robert putting the pressure on their business did them in. Financial hardship is difficult. Just like he's been focused on getting the Hanging H. I had Mackenzie and Justin and you to help with those worries, so I feel like I didn't have quite the burden they did."

"Actually, I've been meaning to talk to you about that."

She looked up at him. "About what?"

"The money that's owed to get your house and place safely paid off. How much is the note?"

"Four hundred thousand dollars."

"So I'd like to pay that off."

Suz's heart dropped. She stared at her husband. "Pay it off?"

"To solve the financial aspect. Get us out from under Donovan."

Suz swallowed hard. "Thank you, I really appreciate the offer. But I can't accept that." Vague discomfort rolled over her that she couldn't place. "Navy SEALs don't make that kind of money. You didn't make any winnings that I know of at rodeo. As you're my husband, I suppose I'm entitled to ask you where you'd get that kind of money." She felt horrible about asking. Didn't want to.

"I have income from the family businesses."

She felt a little sick. "Can we talk about this later? Another time?"

"Sure." He looked at her closely. "I didn't mean to upset you, Suz. I was just thinking about getting Donovan off your back."

"I know," she said softly. "I know you mean well. But the Hanging H is Mackenzie's and mine. It's all we have left of our parents. I don't even know how letting you pay off the note would affect Justin and Mackenzie and their daughters, because you'd own nearly a third of the property outright."

"*We'd* own a third of the property outright, if that's the actual value. But I don't care about that, Suz."

She shook her head. "I thought you were the black sheep, that you don't get along with your family."

"I've been a disappointment to them," he said, his voice careful. "As the eldest son, they expected me to join the family business. When I went into the navy instead, my dad took it real hard. Our relationship was never the same after that. They feel I'm not willing to undertake the family duties. And of course, they're right."

"If that's true, how is it that you have income from your family businesses?"

"They didn't disinherit me. It's not black-and-white like it is in BC. Here if somebody doesn't get along with someone else, you kind of cut each other off."

"That's not entirely true," Suz murmured, realizing for the first time that it really was pretty much that way.

"We're just not close. My family hopes I'll come to my senses at some point." He shrugged. "Which reminds me, I need to call and let them know that our daughters—their granddaughters—have safely arrived in this world."

Suz was really struggling to imagine how one just remembered, several days after their children had been born, to tell their parents. There was a whole family out there of which she'd been unaware who were related to her children—uncles, grandparents. "I don't want their money."

"It's not their money," Cisco said patiently. "It's our money now."

She blinked. "No. It's not. I want the man I married, just the way I married him. No titles, no minor royalty, no family inheritance. Navy SEAL, courageous man, not-so-good rodeo rider. That's the only man I want."

"It doesn't completely work that way. But if you're worried about my family—"

"I'm not worried about your family. I'm worried about you. I need you to be the man I married, not the man I would not have married."

He looked at her. "Suz—"

"Cisco, I'm a small-town girl. You knew what I was. I was happy in the Peace Corps. I would have stayed in, but Mackenzie'd had four babies and she needed me. Plus it was my turn to help run the Hanging H. It was time for me to take responsibility." She took a deep breath. "I'm sorry. I know you're trying to help, but I don't need to be rescued. I'm not looking for a tiara. I'm not Daisy."

"I know that!" He shook his head. "Suz, honey, I know you didn't marry me for any of those things. You didn't know about it."

"I'd be happier if you'd called your family as soon as the babies were born," she said, her heart truly broken. "Cisco, I can't help but feel like you're a little ashamed of us. Maybe not ashamed, but definitely not excited. These are your parents' first grandchildren. Why would you wait days before you called to tell them? Did they even know we were expecting children?" A horrible thought came to her. "Do they know we're married?"

He held up a hand. "Suz, I talk to them once a quarter, approximately. Business meetings, you might call them. That's just the routine, the way it's always been."

"So, no. You didn't break the established routine to tell them you'd gotten married." A little fear crept into her voice. Suz tried to tamp it down. "Why did you marry me knowing I wouldn't fit their standards? Were you just playing rescuer, then, too? SEAL to the rescue?"

"Suz—"

"Like you're trying to save Bridesmaids Creek. And even Daisy. Cisco, saving us isn't going to erase the fact that you're not doing what your family wants you to do. Maybe even needs you to do. And honestly, I didn't sign on for this."

"What are you saying?"

"I don't know what I'm saying." Suz closed her eyes, deeply fearful. "I think I'll go to sleep now. I have to arrange for some cribs or something for the house. I have a couple of things I want to think about," she said quickly, feeling herself retreat into a familiar shell, unable to help herself.

"Do you need me to do anything before I leave? I may go sleep at the bunkhouse tonight, if you want to rest."

"That's a good idea. And no, I don't need anything. Thank you." She didn't open her eyes. It was all too much to think about. She needed to examine why she was suddenly so panicked.

"I'm not ashamed of you and the girls, Suz," he said quietly. "But you're right. I'd rather fit into your world than be part of mine."

She opened her eyes. "You realize the two worlds really don't fit together?"

"They might not, but they will."

Suz looked at her husband, tears in her eyes. She told herself that she was overwhelmed and tired. Tender emotions were normal after a pregnancy.

But they weren't for her, and she knew it. The problem was, she'd married a man who wasn't the man she'd thought he was—and never in her wildest dreams had she ever once wanted the kind of man he was. It sounded horrible, but it was true. She wasn't royalty, she wasn't born with wealth. Her parents had died, chased into an early grave by financial stress and a visitor to their haunted house who'd unfortunately died on their property, ruining their business.

No, she would never have been comfortable marrying into a "very minor royalty" family who didn't get along with their eldest son. She and Mackenzie had always struggled along, knowing they were doing the right thing, but never sure whether the struggle would pay off. To simply marry into money—some kind of aristocratic money—tied to people who could never understand her and would probably never accept her—and that's basically why Cisco had never told his family that he was married—was something she wouldn't have willingly done, had she known.

It wasn't the happily-ever-after ending one dreamed of all their lives, even in the magic-loving, theatrically dramatic, proud little town of Bridesmaids Creek.

Chapter Fourteen

Cisco had stepped in it big-time, and he knew it, but there was very little he could do to change the problem. He was who he was. Suz was just a little worried, that was all, and two weeks after he'd moved her and the babies into the Hanging H, he was ready to move out of the nursery with the hideaway bed and back into his own bed.

He hadn't wanted to push the issue; he'd hoped to be invited to return. But Suz hadn't invited him, and now, even if he did snore on occasion—getting up with babies off and on seemed to bring on a sleep apnea he'd never suffered before—he wanted back in her bed.

Cisco headed out to the porch where Suz was sitting, rocking the babies in a baby swing Cosette had given them, listening to French lullabies. Suz loved the gift, and the babies seemed to really relax and listen to the beautiful music, too. "Good morning."

"Good morning," Suz said, but she didn't look at him. Not the way she'd used to.

He sat on the porch swing next to her. "Suz, we're going to have to work this out."

"I know. I'm trying to."

So maybe he just had to be patient. The problem was,

he wasn't the world's most patient man. Cisco looked at his adorable daughters, peered close to see what they were doing. Just swinging, enjoying the nice day, which was a little warmer than usual for the month of December. Suz had bundled the girls up in white buntings, and they were snugly tucked under pink blankets, with only their little eyes and barely rosy cheeks peeking out. They were so darn cute. How could Suz think he wasn't proud of her and their girls?

Clearly he didn't understand his wife the way he needed to. And now there was a small, yet obvious, canyon between them, which he had to bridge. He didn't want to end up like Cosette and Phillipe. He most certainly didn't want to end up like Phillipe, living in a small house with beads and incense, doing yoga poses, not that there was anything wrong with that. In fact, yoga would probably be very good for him, considering his bull-riding injuries that on occasion—like almost never now—still reminded him of his dunce-like attempts to avoid the lure of BC.

That desire to avoid BC was long in the past. In fact, it was hard to remember why he'd fought BC's charms so hard. Cisco looked around the property, breathing in the peaceful atmosphere. He completely understood why Suz loved it so much; it was a slice of heaven deep in its own special Brigadoon. The house was located several miles outside of Austin, on five hundred acres of land. It was tall and white, Victorian-styled with heavy gingerbreading. Four tall turrets stretched to the sky, and upstairs mullioned windows glinted in the sunlight. A wide wraparound porch painted sky blue held a white wicker sofa with blue cushions, and a collection of wrought-iron roosters sat family-style near a bristly doormat with a big burgundy H on it. Miles and miles of green pastureland, wrapped by white painted pipe fences, adorned the ranch. With around two thousand citizens, BC was a picture postcard in which the Hanging H was the crown jewel.

And he'd been like Robert, he supposed, with his ham-handed rush to try to resolve the Hanging H and its vaunted haunted house for Suz. Robert wanted this piece of property—and as Suz had pointed out, if Cisco paid off the mortgage, he'd be the de facto owner of it. He hadn't really thought through all the particulars of his offer. But the truth was, she hadn't known anything about him. And once she had, she hadn't wanted anything of his.

He couldn't blame her. Even he didn't want to be much of a part of his family. Of course Suz wouldn't want to feel beholden to them in any way—although that wasn't the way he'd intended it.

He had to tell her, explain his feelings to her. They had to get back to the place they'd been before, when it was just the two of them against the world, against the Donovans, against anything that worked to keep them apart. Even BC charms and legends.

A motorcycle roared up the drive, and Cisco realized the time to make up with his wife wasn't going to happen anytime soon. "Here comes trouble."

Suz got up. "I prefer to think of Daisy as an opportunity to learn better people skills."

He hoped he could be so generous. He still hadn't forgiven her for the crazy charms Daisy had given his girls. The dirt and the Bridesmaids Creek water was long gone, dispensed capably no doubt by Cosette and Jane Chatham. He hadn't forgiven her for the photos, either. He was darn lucky he was married to such a confident, spunky woman like Suz.

But for him, the resentment remained.

"Hello!" Daisy exclaimed, bounding up on the porch.

"Hi, Daisy," Suz said, and Cisco nodded curtly, resisting the desire to snatch his children protectively to him and take them inside the house.

Daisy sank onto a chair, gazing over into the baby swing. "Aren't they the cutest things?"

"Daisy, why are you here?" Suz asked.

"Squint said you needed me." Daisy's gaze was on the two girls, seemingly enchanted by them.

"Needed you?" Suz asked.

"Yes. He came to find me." She turned her gaze to smile at Suz and Cisco. "He said you needed help. And so I said I'd come back to see what I could do."

Suz glanced at Cisco, and he couldn't quite meet her inquiring glance.

"Oh, I see," Suz said, and Cisco winced a little. His wife had figured him out a little too quickly. He grinned at her sheepishly.

She raised a brow at him, letting him know that, later on, they'd discuss this new angle. "I could use some help, Daisy. There's a lot to do around the Hanging H."

Daisy rose. "I'm happy to help out for as long as you need me. Let me park my bike in the barn. I hear snow is on the way. And freezing temps."

Daisy headed off, and Suz looked at him. "Freezing temps are indeed on the way."

"Let me try to head them off," Cisco said. "You're the one who said we needed to let bygones be bygones. In fact, I've been hearing that a lot all over this town. So I decided maybe we'd be well-served by adhering to that particular advice. *I'd* be well served by it. Or, to be more honest, I'm living by the keep-your-friends-close-your-enemies-closer rule. It seems best in this town." He sat down next to her. "However, being in the dog-house with you isn't my favorite haunt, so I hope you know that I wanted Daisy back here so we could neu-tralize her. Call me crazy, but I believe that she's our best weapon against Robert."

"Maybe." Suz seemed to consider that. "Don't bring up haunting. It doesn't feel the same around here now that we've closed the Haunted H again."

"It's just until we get Donovan to give up on the idea of buying this place." He looked around, taking in every detail of the wonderful farm. "Listen, Suz, I'm sorry as hell I mentioned paying off the loan. I was trying to help, but I totally see how it would seem like I was pulling a Donovan of my own."

"I overreacted. But I've always figured I could solve my own problems. You're my prince for trying to help, though. Absolutely my prince."

He wasn't much of a prince. And Suz was a lot less annoyed than he figured she might be with his excuse to get Daisy back in Bridesmaids Creek. The truth was, Squint needed a reason to be chasing after her, so he didn't appear like a love-struck hothead—which he was, in the nicest way. It was embarrassing, really, to see his buddy gone all to mush over the town wild child. But there wasn't any changing that particular reality, so Cisco figured they'd all just have to hang on for the ride.

On the other hand, he didn't really know what he was going to do with Daisy now that she was part of their responsibility. His wife was taking that very well. Didn't seem angry in the least.

In fact, if anything, he'd sensed a distinct warming on her part from the second she'd realized he was behind Daisy's sudden return home. She had, after all, wanted him to go after Daisy.

Maybe he wasn't going to end up with a tiny hut next to Phillipe's, with multicolored beads hanging in the doorways and Birkenstocks on his feet. Yet Phillipe would rather be with Cosette in her warm, darling home, Cisco felt certain.

And I don't want to be anywhere but with Suz and my daughters. Even if I have to live the BC way—sucking up to every snake charmer and fake fortune-teller around.

SUZ LEFT THE babies and went into the kitchen, Daisy following close at her heels. Cisco wasn't telling all behind the reappearance of Daisy—she wouldn't have returned to BC just to "help out" with the babies. Not while Daisy was so angry with Cisco's ruination of her chance at BC's magic, her big moment in the sun. And not while Daisy and her father were threatening to take over as much of BC as they possibly could.

No, there was more to the story. Her handsome husband hadn't told all.

"So, what really brings you back to BC?" Suz asked.

Daisy took a bar stool, smiled at Suz. "Cisco said you needed help. Well, he sent that message through Squint. So here I am."

"Where's Squint?" Suz found it highly unlikely that Squint, as hot for Daisy as he was, wouldn't be here right now.

"He stayed at Branch's place."

"Do they even know each other?"

"They know *of* each other, is how I understand the story. Branch is a really nice guy. He probably needed to finish whatever Cisco didn't get done there."

Suz felt herself bristling slightly. "I'm sure Cisco wouldn't have left—"

"Oh, he had to leave. He'd just learned you were pregnant."

"I'm still waiting to hear why you felt like you needed to be the one to tell him."

Daisy lifted her chin. "Look, Suz, you have every right to be mad. I was convinced for a long time that Cisco was supposed to be mine. That once again you'd stolen something that was meant for me. I wasted three chances on Cisco."

"And so? What's changed?"

Daisy shrugged. "I'm going back to Montana to be with Branch as soon as you're squarely on your feet and don't need any more help with the babies."

"I don't— Did you hear something?" Suz looked at Daisy.

Daisy shrugged. "Wind? The news said snow was on the way."

Suz walked into the front room and peeked out to check on Cisco and the babies. He was snoozing under his hat, and the babies slept snugly, tucked up under each of his arms like tiny footballs wrapped in pink blankets. "Maybe I was just hearing things."

Daisy followed her back into the kitchen. "Mommy hormones. Makes you jumpy, probably."

She didn't feel jumpy, she felt a tingle of apprehension she couldn't explain. Justin and Mackenzie had taken their four babies into town for some early Christmas shopping, so the house was empty except for her and Daisy.

Suz plunked down a glass of tea for Daisy as it felt like the right thing to do. "I just have a feeling you're here for a reason you're not sharing."

"Okay," Daisy said. "The honest truth is that Squint asking me to come back here opened up a chance to tell you something that's been on my mind."

"All right." Suz tried not to worry about what might pop out of Daisy's mouth. "I'm listening."

Daisy shook her long locks, fixed the leather skirt that gave her a gypsy-like appearance. "I never really wanted Cisco. I'm glad he's yours."

Suz stared. "I hope you won't be offended when I say I'm dumbfounded to hear you say that."

"I knew you would be. But I think it's important to tell you the truth. The three chances at the magic I had were right. As they always have been. Cisco isn't my kind of guy at all. The magic knew that."

"I don't know what to say." Suz thought quickly, wondering if there was a trap she couldn't see. "How did you come to this realization?"

"It was Branch who helped me see it," Daisy said, sounding a little humble. It was the first time Suz had ever heard that particular tone in her voice. "He's such a loner that he has lots of time to think deeply about stuff. He listened to my situation, and pointed out the obvious that I was too stubborn to see."

"I must meet this miracle of introspection one day," Suz murmured. If the man had actually steered Daisy—stubborn, wild Daisy—onto a new path, he was clearly some kind of amazing muse.

"I'm going back as soon as I can. There's a lot of

things in my life I'm working out, and Branch provides a new perspective."

"I'm so happy for you, Daisy." Suz hardly knew what to think of the changes she saw in her. "Do you have a soft spot for Branch?"

"Oh, no." Daisy laughed again, the sound happy and carefree. "Once upon a time, I thought he might have been falling for me. But then I realized Branch isn't that way. His place is a refuge for many people. Even Cisco went there for sanctuary at one point."

"I know," Suz said, not wanting to be reminded of the time they'd spent apart.

"He just sees things differently. I felt sort of stuck in my life. Branch freed me. And then it hit me that I'd just wanted Cisco in a competitive sort of way. The way I feel like I've always competed with you and Mackenzie and Jade." She smiled, and Suz couldn't detect any snark in her expression. "I don't think it's any secret that I've never felt like I fit in Bridesmaids Creek."

Suz nodded. "I know. You're being very honest, and I really appreciate that." Cisco walked in, both babies in his arms, and Suz smiled at her husband. "Ready for a break?"

"Nope. The babies are happy, I'm happy. I'm going to go sit by the fire in the family room with my girls and enjoy the Christmas tree. Can I talk you into getting me a plate loaded with Christmas cookies?"

"Sure." Suz smiled and got up, placed a few cookies on a plate. After a second's thought, she made a plate for Daisy, too.

"Thank you," Daisy said, sounding surprised.

"So now what will you do?" Suz asked.

"I'm going to ride my motorcycle across the United States. I'd like to see both coasts and parts in between."

"Won't that bother your father? He seemed very upset that you were going back to Montana."

Daisy looked at her. "Suz, I love my father. But the fact is, it's time for some space."

Suz hesitated in the act of taking the plate of cookies and a cup of cocoa to Cisco. "Can you hold that thought? I'll be right back."

She scurried off to deliver the snack to Cisco. He was sexily arranged with both babies near him in their Moses baskets, had a cheery fire going and was reading a book—as if he wasn't concerned in the least that something weird was happening in the kitchen.

"Somebody's kidnapped Daisy," Suz whispered in a rush.

He smiled. "You wish."

"No, I'm serious. There's a body in the kitchen, and it talks and looks like Daisy—but I promise you, it's not the Daisy we know and haven't always loved."

"So give her a chance. Change is forced on all of us sooner or later. It's up to us to make those changes positive or negative."

"Santa Philosopher," Suz muttered, dropping a kiss on his forehead. "Okay, but don't say I didn't warn you. The woman who wants my property and to raze BC to the ground is in my kitchen, and there's a great possibility she's trying to lure me into a sense of false security."

He smiled again. "I'll send in the troops if I begin to sense that you can't handle the situation. But I suspect you have it under control."

"All fine and good for the man relaxing with my darling angels."

"Which I found out about courtesy of Daisy. She has her good points," Cisco said, winking.

"Really not appropriate to remind me of my one transgression." She smiled at her children, kissed Cisco one last time and hurried back into the kitchen. Daisy sat perched on the stool where she'd been before, looking through the sketches of Christmas cookies Betty had brought over.

"These are pretty. Some of these are works of art," Daisy said. She turned a page in the photo book. "Betty could go national with these cookies."

"I don't know if Betty and Jade have ever considered anything grander than selling their delicacies in BC." Suz plunked down on a stool, took a deep breath. "So you were telling me about this trip you'd like to take."

Daisy nodded. "It's time for space. I've thought a lot about my life, and Branch made me realize I've never been out of BC. Not since I came here. I know you haven't, either," Daisy said quickly, "but this is your hometown."

"It's yours, too."

"Not as much. I'm not a native daughter. Branch mentioned that if I'd gone away to college, or lived in another place, I might feel more like I have a place in the world."

"Does your dad know you want to travel?"

"He doesn't yet. I was still pondering Branch's observations when Squint came after me and told me you needed me. Frankly, that was music to my ears. So after I help out here, I'll take my trip. I'll head to Branch's, then see the rest of the country." She smiled. "Just tell me what you need me to do."

Suz shifted uncomfortably, thinking fast. She didn't

want to stamp out the kindness that was blossoming in Daisy, because that would be wrong. Suz knew she herself wouldn't feel very good if she offered in good faith to make amends—which she sincerely felt Daisy was trying to do—and was turned down. "There's so much to do around here," Suz said, going for the non-committal, which just happened to be the truth. "Daisy, Squint was right. We need help on every level. You could pretty much pick your project. How long are you planning to stay in BC?"

"Until after Christmas. That gives me time to break the news gently to Dad after the holidays. I worry about him, you know."

Suz thought she'd never known a man who required worry less, but kept her opinion on that to herself. All her thoughts had to go toward what she could put Daisy in charge of. It was a sticky question. "One thing I could really use some help with is scouting a place for Cisco and me and the girls to live. Some place small," Suz said quickly. "Very small. Quaint, too."

"It can't be too small, you have two babies."

"True." But she was still a little rattled by Cisco's offer to pay off their note and mortgage. She didn't want him to do that—but she wasn't going to be working for a while so her options to earn were a little limited. "But I'm being careful of my finances until I can work again."

Daisy looked at her. "Suz, I know very well Cisco's family is quite wealthy."

"What does that mean to me?" Suz asked stiffly.

Daisy shrugged. "Nothing, I guess. So, maybe twenty-five hundred square feet for your new home?"

"That would be perfect. Or even a little less." The

more Suz thought about it, the more she warmed to the idea of Daisy doing their house hunting for them. She and her father knew plenty about the properties in the town. And Cisco could do it, but this would keep Daisy busy and useful.

"You know Madame Matchmaker's place is on the market?" Daisy asked.

Suz froze. "I could never buy their house. I'm still hoping they get back together."

Daisy nodded. "Me, too."

Nothing could have shocked Suz more. "Do you mean that?"

"Of course I do! I never wanted them to split up! Who would want that on their conscience?"

Suz sat dumbfounded. "Daisy, you amaze me."

Daisy shook her head. "Them splitting up is bad for me, Suz. I still want my turn at the magic. I don't know how I'm going to get that turn, but I know a happy matchmaker is a matchmaker who's paying attention to her job."

"Ohh." Suz wholeheartedly agreed with that sentiment.

"The Martin place is on the market."

Suz went completely still. "It's been on the market for years."

Daisy nodded. "Because it's supposed to be haunted. But you've made your living on ghost stories. I think moving into an actual haunted house would even improve your street cred for running the local haunted house."

Suz didn't dare breathe. It felt like an iron band was tightening around her chest. Daisy made it sound like there would continue to be a Haunted H. Could this new Daisy be for real? Did a trip to Montana change a woman so completely? Even give her a heart and a soul?

Suz sipped her cocoa while Daisy munched thoughtfully on a frosted reindeer cookie. Cisco wandered into the kitchen, hitched himself onto a stool. "My daughters are napping like angels. It's amazing how well they sleep," he said proudly. "Like tiny dolls. I put the monitor right by their baskets."

Of course they weren't more than twenty feet from the babies, but Suz still flipped on the monitor in the kitchen, anyway. "Cisco, Daisy suggests we might want to look at the Martin place."

He looked at Suz. "Is that the house that's really haunted? Not like the Haunted H, but actually, truly possessing ghostly activity?"

Suz laughed. "I don't know that it's been verified."

"You mean with a ghostbusting team," Cisco said, and Suz knew he was teasing.

"I suppose it's silly. But I can't help but hesitate," Suz said. "The ghosts that live there appear to be early settlers to the town who didn't make it with their ranching business. But they wouldn't give up and sell, either, so eventually they were never seen again. Rumor has it—"

"Further rumor," Cisco interjected.

"Yes, further rumor is that the reason they were so reluctant to leave is that they were love-struck bank robbers."

Cisco grinned. "Love-struck bank robbers who couldn't keep up with their small house and property on which they were running cattle that wouldn't turn profitable for them?"

"Suz has the story right. I know it sounds silly, but that's been the tale forever. It was one of the first stories I heard when I came to BC, and it sort of gave me the willies." Daisy held up a cookie decorated like a Christmas tree, studying it. "I still say these cookies are works of art."

Cisco shrugged, still smiling. Suz could tell he wasn't taking any of the story seriously. "So we don't look at the Martin place. We'll find someplace else."

"If you could talk Dad into not buying your house and business, you could build a small place at the Hanging H," Daisy said, and Suz nearly fell off her stool.

Chapter Fifteen

Suz glanced at Cisco, stunned. That tight feeling around her chest was back—she didn't dare hope that there was such a change in Daisy. "Daisy, you're not suggesting there's a possibility your father could be persuaded to change his mind about calling the liens on our property?"

Daisy put the cookie down. "It would be good for Dad to slow down a little. He needs to enjoy life. I really worry about his heart, ever since he had that cardiac event."

"It was a scary time." Suz remembered how angry and convinced Daisy had been that events at the Hanging H had caused her father's health troubles. It wasn't true, of course; Robert Donovan had a mean streak a mile wide, and he was determined to build an empire on the back of BC.

Or he had been. Even Mr. Donovan had been showing signs of softening lately—witness his dread that his only daughter might move off to Montana with a man, never to return. Robert was more scared of that than anything.

Still, Daisy hated the idea that the magic had passed her by. She honestly believed in what BC had to offer.

That could only mean one thing: she could still join their side, even against her father's position. But Robert would win, too, if his daughter stayed in Bridesmaids Creek.

"You know, Daisy," Suz said, "have you ever considered becoming a matchmaker?"

Cisco and Daisy both stared at her. The silence in the room was of the astounded variety. "Well, have you?" Suz asked. Cisco's gaze was on her, and though she knew she'd caught him totally off guard, there was a twinkle forming in his eyes.

"No, I haven't. I was focused on finding my own match, I suppose." Daisy looked from Suz to Cisco and back again. "Cosette has always been our matchmaker."

"Yes, she has. But the thing is, Cosette's going through her own rough time."

"That's true," Daisy said thoughtfully.

"It wouldn't surprise me if Cosette was looking for an apprentice," Cisco said.

Suz smiled at her husband gratefully. "We could talk to her. Daisy would be a perfect apprentice. And then, Daisy, you'd still have a chance at the magic."

"Do you think so?" Daisy looked as if she were almost afraid to believe.

"I'm almost positive—" Suz stopped as the back door opened. Daisy's gang of five trooped in, making themselves at home, followed by Betty Harper.

"Look who I found outside holding down the ground," Betty said. "They looked hungry, so I invited them in."

Daisy sat straight up, staring at her gang. She considered Dig, Carson, Clint, Red and Gabriel. "I know exactly where I'm starting if Suz's wild-eyed plan for making me a matchmaker actually takes off."

Suz and Cisco glanced at each other—then her sexy husband winked at her.

Oh, the plan was going to take off—like a military jet, if her husband had anything to do with it. Suz could tell by the look in Cisco's eyes that the plan of putting Daisy in veritable charge of Bridesmaids Creek was one that met with his complete approval.

It was going to happen sooner or later—at least this way, with Daisy in charge, it pitted Robert against the daughter he loved so dearly.

CISCO PONDERED THE five knuckleheads who'd just invaded their kitchen like lost lambs looking for their shepherdess. Daisy didn't seem all that happy to see her gang, a development that caught Cisco's attention. Meanwhile Suz sat calmly at the table, spinning what he thought was a brilliant plan of action.

He admired his wife's ability to think on her feet, especially when surrounded by the enemy. "What's going on, fellows? Thought you were hanging out down at the creek with Sam."

"Yeah. We were." Dig glanced at Daisy. "But he's going to be there a long time. Says he's used to living under adverse conditions, and that our creek is quite comfortable. He'd caught a couple of fish and was roasting them on a nice fire when we left. Had a great little fire pit thing going."

"Ah. Too rustic for you?" Cisco asked. He knew Sam too well. Sam could stay out there for a few years living like Grizzly Adams. Eventually, it would be hard to find him. He'd melt into the landscape like a shadow, become one with the forest. There was actually some urgency to getting his buddy out of his "camping" zone before the situation went past comfortable for all.

"A little bit," Red spoke up. "He's pretty hard-core."

"Yes, he is." And Sam's theory was that the creek couldn't be dammed up and scraped out if someone was legitimately living there. He had to admire Sam for being willing to go the distance for BC. "So you're here for cookies?"

"Sure would be nice." Gabriel put his paw out when the plate of cookies was passed by him. "Thanks, Suz."

"How come you guys never married?" Cisco asked. Daisy and Suz looked at him, surprised, then waited to hear the answer.

"Well, Gabriel always sort of hoped Daisy might have a soft spot for him," Clint said.

"Me! It was Dig!" Gabriel exclaimed.

Dig glanced around, embarrassed. "Carson is the fellow who never stopped making calf's eyes at you, Daisy."

Carson stopped in the middle of snacking on a peppermint-stick-shaped cookie. "It was Red who had hearts in his eyes every time Daisy got within three miles of him. Went all gooey, like marshmallows over a fire."

All the men in Daisy's gang had turned a shade that spoke to their true feelings. "Let me get this straight," Cisco said, "you're all in love with Daisy?"

The five men slowly nodded sheepishly.

"She always was the town's best girl," Dig said.

Daisy gasped. *"Me?"*

Cisco glanced over at Suz, who was smiling at him like he was the best thing since homemade cookies.

He really liked that look in her eyes—and if he had his way, that look was going to be there every day of their lives together.

"*I* was the town's best girl?" Daisy asked.

"Who did you think it was?" Clint asked, seemingly truly mystified.

"Well, I thought…" Daisy began, glancing at Suz, but Suz pulled out the pot to make more cocoa.

"Anybody in the mood for a mug of Betty Harper's delicious, practically county-renowned cocoa?" Suz asked, interrupting Daisy before she could knock the glow off her own big moment.

"I'd love to make up a big pot of cocoa," Betty said, commandeering a pot and the cocoa fixings from the cabinet. "Who's up for some?"

All the men raised their hands eagerly. Cisco thought he'd never seen a group led to pasture so willingly. This was going to be easy—and then he was going to have Suz all to himself. Just him and Suz and their daughters—the thought made him happier than anything he could have ever imagined. He was so much in love with Suz that the thought of spending the rest of his life with her made him grin from ear to ear. Which he'd always thought was a totally clichéd expression—until he'd experienced the fact that one could indeed stop what they were doing in the middle of the day and realize they had a grin on their face that just wouldn't quit. Between Suz and their daughters—well, the smile had become a permanent fixture on his face.

Mackenzie walked into the kitchen holding documents in her hands, which were trembling. "Daisy, what are you doing here?"

"I'm helping out." The smile that had been on Daisy's

face from her gang admitting they were love-struck for her slid off. "What's wrong?"

Mackenzie looked around at everyone in the kitchen. "Suz, can I see you for a moment?"

The room went silent. Cisco suddenly had a horrible feeling he knew what Mackenzie was holding. He got up, helped Suz to her feet to follow her sister into the family room. The babies still slept silently, peacefully unaware of anything but that they were loved. Five feet away from them, Mackenzie took a deep breath, handed her sister the document.

"We're out," Mackenzie said. "It's over, Suz."

Suz was absolutely still, so Cisco took the papers from Mackenzie, reading them quickly.

Sure enough, the foreclosure was final. Cisco felt sick, sick at heart, sick in his soul. Justin walked in, coming to stand behind Mackenzie, putting his arms around his distraught wife. Suz stayed totally motionless, but when Cisco pulled her gently into his arms, she came willingly to rest against his chest.

He'd never felt so helpless in his life.

And there was nothing he could do to help now.

It was the worst feeling he'd ever experienced, and the knowledge that his wife had lost the home that meant so much to her, the place where she'd dreamed of her own children growing up, broke his heart.

SUZ WENT BACK into the kitchen silently, thinking to shoo off Daisy's gang, and Daisy, too, so that she and Cisco could think through a plan for their future, which had suddenly, drastically changed. Her heart was shattered at the knowledge that the home where she and Mackenzie had grown up, known so many happy times, was lost to them. That her children would never know the heartwarming joy of the Hanging H devastated her. Somehow, she still felt her parents here, their love and belief in their daughters, and all the wonderful days they'd spent in their family home. All gone now.

She'd stepped back into the kitchen to say that, for this evening, the Hanging H was uncustomarily closing its doors to visitors, but everyone was gone, even Betty, leaving behind a pot of warm cocoa and a sparkling clean island top, the cookies put away. Daisy remained, perched on a kitchen stool, her shoulders slumped.

"I'm so sorry, Suz. I'm about to leave, I know I'm the last person you want to see right now." She pointed to the monitor. "I'm afraid we all heard accidentally. By the time I'd handed it to Betty and she'd turned it off, we had a pretty good gist of what was going on." Tears sparkled in Daisy's eyes. "I'll talk to Dad. That's all I want you to know." She took a deep breath and rose from the stool. "I don't know if I can do anything, because Dad's stubborn when he gets his mind to something. But I'll try."

Suz hardly knew what to say. Her throat closed up hard. She watched as Daisy walked out, realizing as the door closed that something about Daisy seemed wildly different.

She seemed *sincere.* As if she really cared about the Hanging H and their family. Suz poured some of the cocoa for herself, nibbled disconsolately on a frosted cookie shaped like a Christmas tree. She was so stunned by everything she couldn't even cry. Cisco came in, sat on the stool next to her, and she poured him a mug of cocoa, too.

"I'm sorry as hell, Suz." His voice was so rough with emotion Suz knew he was feeling everything she was.

"It's all right. It's my own fault. I should have accepted your help when you offered." She took another deep breath. "I'm stubborn, Cisco. I've always been stubborn. It's gotten me through the toughest times in my life. But today I learned there's stubborn, and then there's too stubborn."

"Jesus, Suz."

He turned on the stool and pulled her into his arms, and then she did cry, big, fat, overwhelmed tears that shook her. The more he held her, the safer she felt, and so she let it all pour out of her, until she'd cried what felt like every last tear in her reservoir. All the sorrow, worry and pain of the past months' anxiety about the foreclosure poured out of her, draining her.

"Thank goodness for Betty's cocoa," Suz said, sniffling out an embarrassed laugh as she tried to make light of her tears. She failed miserably. "I guess Robert finally won. He was patient, and he won."

"I wish there was something I could do," Cisco said, and she could tell he felt helpless, so she forced herself to blow her nose and pour some steel into her spine.

"There's nothing anyone can do. Mackenzie and I got outmaneuvered, that's all." She tossed her tissues away, washed her hands and face at the sink. "The whole town knows by now. The baby monitor was on, and before Betty could turn it off, of course Daisy and her gang had heard." The whole town where you'd grown up knowing you'd lost your house wasn't the world's most comforting thought—but it probably didn't matter, anyway. They would have found out soon enough.

"Did they all just leave?"

"They evaporated pretty quickly on hearing the news. But Daisy hung around." She looked out at the gently falling snow, arriving just as forecast. "Our first snow of the season," she said softly, somehow cheered in spite of herself.

"What did she have to say?"

"That she'd talk to her father." Suz shrugged. "But I'm not sure even Daisy can change Robert's mind. He's wanted this place for so long. It's the crown jewel of his desires."

"I'd like to kick his greedy tail, but I don't think it would solve anything. It'd feel great, though."

Suz went back to her stool. "Well, we don't have to vacate for a month. That means we'll have one Christmas here with the babies." She smiled at Cisco. "That's something, isn't it?"

He pulled her into his arms, and then edged her up into his lap, holding her as if he were afraid she, too, might disappear, just like their dreams, and the house, if he let her go. Suz rested there against his chest and closed her eyes, feeling safe in spite of not knowing what the future held.

Maybe she should have let Cisco help them out. That would have solved everything, she supposed.

But she didn't regret that decision—not even now, knowing that they'd lost their parents' beloved ranch and business. She hadn't known he was some kind of charmed prince when she'd married him, and she probably wouldn't have married him, anyway, if she'd known she'd bring a bankruptcy and foreclosure to the marriage.

Mackenzie had agreed with her when she'd told her of Cisco's generous offer.

In her heart, she knew she'd been a little selfish not to take help, but what had been the other option? In forty years, maybe the Haunted H might have made enough money to cover a four hundred thousand dollar payback to her husband. But she would have always felt somehow daunted, held back, by the size of that loan. She would have always felt like he'd saved her.

What she wanted was an equal partnership with a husband, not a rescuing prince on a white steed riding in to save the day. Save her.

Stubborn she would have to remain.

It's gotten me this far, she thought. *Stubborn Suz will just have to figure this out the same way she always has.*

Stubbornly.

CISCO WAS THUNDERSTRUCK enough by the alarming turn of events of the evening to sneak off after he'd put Suz to bed. He made sure the babies were tucked cozily in with their mother, which was the way she preferred to sleep at night while she was still nursing. On occasion, he slept in the bed so he could help Suz with the nursing and diapering—but he never really slept. He was pretty certain he wouldn't roll over and squish a baby, but for the better sake of valor, he'd had a cot moved in. Therefore, he slept right beside Suz, and the babies slept beside her, completely surrounded by king-size pillows to block them from rolling out. He'd sleep on the cot a while longer, until his wife told him it was safe to come back to their bed.

Suz was tired after nursing, and he'd been glad to see her relaxing. He'd murmured that he was going out for a while, and she'd answered with a sleepy, "'K," so he'd felt fine about heading off.

He needed to chew the fat the way he'd never needed to before. And the only man who could chew the fat for hours and still be stocked full of gab, was Handsome Sam.

Finding his buddy wasn't going to be an easy feat. No doubt he'd have moved camp by now, because once a SEAL, always a SEAL. Besides, so many people knew where Sam was that his campsite had become a regular draw for the sheriff, Daisy's gang, even Phillipe, who had left his beads and yoga for a bit to visit with Sam. People liked Sam because he was a glib charmer—on the surface. Only his SEAL brothers knew that Sam was anything but the quixotic hero he presented to the world. He and Squint were a lot alike in that regard: kind, easygoing—dangerous.

He slipped through some bushes and overgrowth, and as he'd suspected, Sam had departed. "Sam!" he yelled, not caring to be silent.

"Right behind you."

Cisco rolled his eyes. "I heard you. You're not as sneaky as you used to be."

Sam laughed. "Says you. Come visit my humble abode."

"Why'd you move?" he asked, following his buddy.

"You know exactly why. This is Bridesmaids Creek. A man can't get any peace around here. Everyone's so darn friendly."

"Yeah. I've gotten used to it, though."

They slunk deeper into the forest until Sam stopped in front of a large oak tree that looked ghostly and somber in the moonlight. "Are you living in it, or under it?" Cisco admired the huge live oak that seemed to stretch its canopy for a mile in all directions.

"The ground's fine for me. Stretch out and I'll share the fish I grilled."

"You go ahead. I'm stuffed full of Christmas cookies and cocoa. I brought you some, by the way."

"I know. I can smell them. Hand them over." Sam appreciatively grabbed the bag. "And the thermos of cocoa, please."

Cisco laughed. "Betty's homemade."

"I'm not sharing, so I hope you brought yourself a water bottle."

"Not very companionable of you." Cisco leaned against the tree trunk, surveying Sam's new domain. "You staking a claim out here to keep Robert Donovan from bringing in ditch witches and other earth-moving equipment may not be such a wild-eyed idea."

"Oh?" Sam barely looked up from his inspection of the pretty cookies he was examining by the light of his headlamp.

"He's managed to buy the Hanging H and, by default of course, the Haunted H."

Sam's head jerked up. "When did that happen?"

"Mackenzie and Suz got the papers tonight. It wasn't the most fun moment. Be glad you missed out on it."

"There's nothing that can be done?"

"Nope. It's over. Airtight. Foreclosed on and sold outright."

"Thought those things should take a few months to get through the banks."

"Not when you own the banks." Cisco put his wrists on his knees, pondered the nearly empty sky. Only a full moon bloomed in an otherwise starless night. Snow filtered down in small, insubstantial flurries, not doing more than dusting the ground. Below the huge canopy, they were completely dry. "Anyway, I guess the earth moves for a rich man."

"You're a rich man," Sam said quietly.

"My wife didn't want my help." It still stung his pride a bit, but he'd understood Suz's feelings. He wouldn't want to take help from anyone, either.

He'd desperately wanted to help his wife, though. Felt like that was what a caring, strong husband did: helped his wife when she needed him. "I wish she had let me help, but, Sam, you and I have our share of stubborn, too."

"So there's nothing to be done."

Cisco shook his head. "Not unless you have an idea."

"Is that why you're here? Not just to bring me cookies and cocoa?" Sam laughed. "What makes you think I have any ideas?"

"Because your mind works differently than the average human's."

Sam laughed again. "You butter me up with Betty's cocoa and Hanging H cookies, and then hint that I'm subhuman. Trust me, I know your brand of flattery."

Cisco moved his hat back, buttoned his sheepskin jacket against the cold. "More like superhuman when it comes to brain juice."

"Thanks."

He hadn't stated anything everyone in the Navy hadn't known. Cisco might have been the swimmer, but Sam had brains to spare and then some.

"Well, if it was me, I'd say you better marry Squint off to Daisy."

Cisco frowned. "That won't be happening. Squint's long gone—"

"Big baby," Sam said. "Hiding out at the first sign of trouble."

"And he's with Branch. Who really appears to have worked a number on Daisy, by the way." He looked thoughtful. "There's no telling what frame of mind Squint may return in." If he ever returned.

"We can always count on Branch to reroute someone's head. Look at what happened to you."

Cisco straightened. "What do you mean?"

"You went off all Mr. Independent. You came home ready to settle down."

He could see Sam grinning at him like a jack-o'-lantern in the firelight. "I made no secret of my feelings for Suz from the start."

"Yeah, but you weren't eager for the altar. Took you getting squished flat by bulls and peacing out at Branch's to make you realize you were chasing the wrong thing."

"Yeah, well. What's your excuse?"

"I'm never settling down. This has been abundantly clear to everyone from the time I was a kid." Sam sighed with happiness as he sipped on the cocoa. "But watching you fall in love and get married was one of the highlights of my life, I'll admit that. A great success, I don't mind saying."

"Like you had anything to do with it." Cisco grunted.

"The artist never reveals the secrets of his chosen medium," Sam said, and Cisco grunted again.

"And yet, lately, I've been wondering if maybe circumventing the BC charms was the beginning of the end," Cisco said.

"I've wondered when you'd see that."

Cisco raised a brow. "You don't mean you believe in the Bridesmaids Creek claptrap?"

"I've been sleeping here for days, haven't I?"

Cisco stared at Sam. Sam's face was devoid of a smile in the firelight. "You're serious."

"Sure I am."

"And you think the chain of disasters that have occurred in Suz's and my life is because I didn't observe the proper customs?"

"It's never wise to circumvent the history of a place. Its tribal traditions are important," Sam said. "Where would we be without observing customs? Societies are built on it, and wisely so."

"So what do I do?" Cisco asked.

"I told you. You have to get Daisy hooked up with Squint."

"What was all that babble about observing customs? Tribal lore and ways?"

"Babble." Sam grinned. "That's what you came for, isn't it?"

Chapter Sixteen

"Sam was no help." Cisco walked into Cosette's small, comfortable house, noticing at once the sweet floral scent of cut flowers. "Maybe no one can help."

"And you hate the feeling that goes along with not being able to help your wife and family." Cosette nodded, pointing him onto a screened porch with plants galore and a couple of lovebirds snugly content in a beautiful cage. "Sit down. We'll think our way through this."

"The thing is," Cisco said, a little amazed when Cosette handed him, not cocoa or tea, which he thought were standards in Bridesmaids Creek, but a healthy tumbler of whiskey, "I love Suz. I'm crazy about her. She's the best thing that's ever happened in my life. But I'm afraid I may have jinxed us. There may be something to this crazy BC lore." He looked at Cosette, comforted by the gentle understanding he saw in her eyes. Her pink-frosted hair shone softly in the light from the two lamps on the porch.

"Well, one can't say for sure. You're talking to a divorced woman." She sat back on a patterned cushion and smiled. "I don't think I'm a good testament to the powers of Bridesmaids Creek anymore."

"But you wouldn't be divorced if it wasn't for Robert Donovan. You'd still have your business, and Phillipe wouldn't be giving yoga lessons in a house with hanging hippie beads for decor."

"If, and were, and wouldn't." Cosette shrugged. "Who knows for sure?"

"I know. Donovan is the closest thing we have here to a bogeyman."

Cosette laughed. "Even bogeymen can be charmed."

"Yeah, well." He sipped at his whiskey, appreciating the warmth of it and the coziness of Cosette's porch. "Not our bogeyman. His daughter has had some strange renaissance, but Donovan never would. You would have thought his coronary event would have softened him, or Jade threatening to keep him away from his granddaughters." He shook his head. "We thought we had him pinned when he signed those papers after Jade held his feet to their fire."

"And yet, held them not long enough, obviously." Cosette sipped her tiny glass of whiskey, thinking. "I don't blame Robert for the end of my marriage. Or losing my business. Not anymore."

"You don't? Because he sure as hell couldn't have helped. Financial stress is hard on a marriage."

"True. But if it's Robert's fault, then why are you still married? Your wife has lost her home and business, too."

He sat straight up, horrified. "You're right."

"I know." Cosette nodded. "Obstacles usually make us stronger. They can, if we let them."

He wasn't sure if he'd been a support or a hindrance to Suz when she was losing the home she dearly loved. "I want my marriage to be a strong one. I love Suz. I adore her. She's given me so much more than I could ever give her."

"Not necessarily. Heroic, but not necessarily true." Cosette pondered that. "What would your family say?"

"About what?"

"About you being virtually homeless with two babies and a wife."

"They'd say—" Cisco thought about that. "They'd say I needed to come home and help with the family business and pull my life back together."

"And would they be right?"

"No. Not at all. I'm where I belong."

She nodded. "*I* know that. And *you* know that. But does Suz?"

He swallowed hard. "I think so. I hope so."

"It's not fairy tales or magic that makes BC. We have magic here, but it's not a step-by-step rubric or even a recipe one can follow. It's just magic. And magic can't be understood."

"Sam says we need to get Daisy and Squint together. I suppose his plan is to either soften Robert's heart up with grandchildren—"

"Which didn't work before."

Cisco nodded. "Or get back the Hanging H that way. Through marriage."

"Which means we'd have to trust Daisy." Cosette looked at him curiously. "That would definitely be going out for the long ball."

"Yeah. Anyway, Sam's dumb." He grunted. "Actually, he's smart as hell. Mensa. But Squint's gone to Montana. He may never come back."

"You did."

He shrugged. "Because I found out I was going to be a father."

"How do you think that makes Suz feel?"

He hesitated. "What do you mean?"

"That you're here because she had babies."

"I married her because I'm in love with her. I want to be with her."

"You even ignored the charms and legends here because you love her. Plotted against them, even. Some might even say you cheated Daisy to win Suz."

"Some might say that, and they'd probably be right. But I didn't mean any harm to Daisy."

"You just didn't believe in the legend."

"No." He shook his head. "No, I didn't."

"But now you want it to work for you."

"It would be nice," he admitted.

"Magic doesn't work that way. You're either willing or not. It doesn't start and stop, or work one day when you want it, and not another day."

He nodded. "I get that now."

"She worked hard for you, Cisco. You know why the magic didn't work for her, neither of the three times?"

"Because I didn't love her. I loved Suz."

"It didn't work because she didn't really want you."

He sipped his whiskey. "That's the only good news I've heard today."

"So have some faith. The magic will work again."

"Maybe, but not in time to get Suz's ranch back." He was mad enough at Robert to punch him in the nose, if he were here right now.

"Maybe it's not your fight," Cosette said softly. "Maybe it's just like Suz told you. She doesn't want your help."

He hesitated. "I'm her husband. I'm supposed to help her."

Cosette smiled gently. "You have a hearing problem, dear man. You hear, but you don't listen. Suz is telling you exactly what she wants and needs. It's exactly the same thing she told you when she wouldn't let you buy the Hanging H. She said she'd handle it."

"You're right." A dawning sense of understanding hit him. "You're absolutely right."

"Sometimes people just need a listening ear and a shoulder to cry on." Cosette rose, covered her lovebirds to carry inside. "I must get to bed. It's an early day for me tomorrow."

"Thank you for the whiskey. And the wisdom," he said, following her into the house.

"No problem." She walked him to the front door. "It will all work out."

At the door, he turned to look down at the small, spare woman he considered a dear friend. "I suppose you'd let me know if there was something I could do to help you and Phillipe."

Cosette smiled. "Phillipe is just fine. He's back in my spare bedroom sleeping." She laughed at the stunned expression on his face. "Let there be some magic in your life, Cisco. It always comes to those who believe in it. Go enjoy Christmas with your family."

"Merry Christmas, Cosette." He kissed her cheek and departed, his mind whirling with everything he'd learned tonight.

At home, the babies were still sound asleep with their mother. Suz opened her eyes when he came in. "You're back."

"Yes. The snow's coming down harder now. I expect

the ground will be covered in the morning. We could even have a white Christmas."

She turned on a soft night-light by the bed. "You must be cold."

"I've been to Cosette's. She warmed me up with some delightful Irish whiskey. Believe me, I'm ready to fight off any chill."

"I figured you'd gone to find Sam."

He pulled off his boots, shucked his jeans and shirt. "Oh, I found him, too."

"He needs to get to the bunkhouse. Jade called to say we're expecting half a foot of snow tomorrow."

Cisco shook his head. "He'll come in when he's ready. Sam's stubborn like that."

"Like someone else I know." He saw Suz watching him intently as he reached his cot. "You look cold," she said.

He stilled. They'd already discussed his body temperature, he'd assured his wife he was fine—

He got it like a thunderbolt. "Oh, I'm very cold. Freezing. About froze my hiney off out there chatting with Grizzly Adams. You know Sam, he's a talker. Couldn't get him to shut up. By the time I could leave, I'm lucky I didn't have frostbite." He looked at her, wondering if he'd sufficiently communicated his desire for her.

She pulled back the covers. "Come get in bed. I'll warm you up."

Briefly he worried about it, wondered if he might hurt her, panicked about squashing the babies.

Oh, hell. Cosette's right. I hear but I don't listen worth a damn.

He jumped straight into bed with his wife, snuggling into Suz's body warmth, the only home he'd ever wanted, right here with her and their babies.

Heaven on earth. And suddenly, Cisco felt the magic he'd been missing for so long.

Suz GOT UP the next morning, kissed her husband, who lay sleeping like a bronze god in her bed, and shrugged on a robe.

"Come back," Cisco said.

Suz smiled at him. "I'm going to let you sleep a little longer."

"I'm wide awake." He sat up. "I don't know if I've ever told you this, Suz, but I love the hell out of you."

"I love you, too. And our girls love you."

"And well they should. I'm a girls' daddy. You've heard of daddy's girls? Well, these little ones," he said, peeking over into their baskets, "have a girls' daddy."

"I always suspected you had a soft heart for women," Suz teased. "I'm going to feed them, and then I'm going out for a while. Would you mind watching them?"

"Would I mind watching my daughters? Do people plot in BC? Do bears scratch their furry butts on trees?" He watched her as she picked up a baby. "My girls are always going to know the kind of support I never had."

Suz looked at him as she sat down to nurse. "You never really mentioned you didn't feel supported by your family. Just that you didn't care to go into the family business."

He shrugged. "It wasn't a popular decision to become a SEAL. My family never threatened to disown me or cut me out of the line of—"

Suz had a terrible thought. "Whatever minor royalty you are, please don't say it. I don't want to know."

She had a feeling Daisy knew quite well, but Suz had no such curiosity of her own. "Promise me you'll never tell our girls that they come from any kind of whatever royalty you are."

He looked sad. "I really can't do that. It's not something you can exactly get away from."

"You did."

"Not totally."

She gazed at his face, reading something there she didn't want to see. "Oh, no. Cisco, I thought that because you aren't on good terms with your family that you had no responsibility to your whatever you are." She gulped. "I have to warn you, I'm not the kind of girl to wear a tiara. You probably knew that when you met me with blue hair and a nose stud."

He smiled. "I do know that about you, but it doesn't change that the little girls are ladies."

She swallowed hard. "No. Tell them we don't want it. We don't do those kinds of things here, Cisco. We're Bridesmaids Creek. We cheer for and back our own when one of us succeeds, like when Ty made it into BUD/S and then got his Trident. We're proud of our hometown heroes. But we're homegrown here. We don't put on airs and tiaras and whatever else."

"I know how you feel, because I've hidden from it myself. But I've ignored it as long as I can. I'm the eldest, and when my father passes away, I'll be head of our estate."

She realized she was holding her baby as if she might disappear. Her whole world was changing. There was no way to stop what was happening. "I wish you would have told me in the beginning."

"Before we got married."

"Yes." Suz nodded. "Absolutely before we got married. I had a right to know. And you knew I wouldn't be comfortable with anything like this."

"You asked me for a child, Suz, and at the time, that was pretty much all I could take in," he said quietly. "Regardless, the babies have some claim to the estates."

"But they wouldn't have been any kind of 'minor' royalty. The only royalty they should ever have to think about is being homecoming queens and Bridesmaids Creek princesses." She felt herself getting angry, because now she had nothing, and she felt strange, like their marriage had become unbalanced. She'd never wanted anything from anyone—and now she had no land, no ranch, no house, even, to offer in the marriage.

Suddenly, she realized how Cosette and Phillipe must have felt, a little, when their marriage had become unbalanced. "Promise me you'll never tell the girls."

"I can't. They'll have to be presented, Suz."

She shook her head. "It's not right. It's not fair. That's too much to put on two small-town girls who deserve to grow up just the same way I did. Breathing small-town air, getting to know each member of the community and caring about them every single day and rejoicing when they do well, cry when they suffer setbacks. But always being part of the fabric of this wonderful town."

"Which just might not be here forever, Suz," he said quietly, and she couldn't help herself from the sudden tears that slipped from her eyes. She wiped them away impatiently.

"Of course BC is always going to be here. It's going to take more than Robert Donovan to destroy us." She was determined about that.

He tried to talk to her some more, but her mind was

on last night, and how wonderful it had felt to hold Cisco again. She intended to keep her marriage. *They don't call me Stubborn Suz for nothing.*

She had to change the shape of destiny enveloping their town. Only then could she feel like she had her powers back, her sense of value and self-worth that only came—for her—from owning a place that her parents had built with their own dreams and hard work. Cisco had tried to help, but he had his own heritage to think of, and besides which, nobody could save her but her.

She laid the babies quietly in the bed with their father, kissed them both.

"I'll take mine, too," he said, "right here." He pointed to his mouth, and she was only too happy to kiss him.

She wasn't running.

She was going to stand and fight for everything that was Bridesmaids Creek, the Hanging H, and most of all, her husband and the miraculous babies they'd made together.

Just to be sure he understood her intentions, she kissed Cisco again, until he felt the special magic that only the two of them shared.

Suz had never been inside the Donovan home. To her memory, no one she knew had. The gray-stoned mansion rose up on the land like an enormous fairy cake that had overbaked its pan. An arch at the end of the drive showcased a massive D—just in case anyone didn't know this was the Donovan compound.

Of course everyone knew who lived here. It was practically shouted from the second-story rooftop with opulence everywhere, from the marble fountain in the center of the circle drive to the six chimneys rimmed with gray stone above. Massive arched double doors welcomed visitors to the front of the house, and a white-gloved butler opened the front door. She could see a white-aproned housekeeper dusting a twinkling chandelier in the foyer.

"May I help you?" the butler asked.

"I'd like to see Daisy Donovan, if I could, please."

"Whom shall I say is calling?"

"Suz Grant." Suz looked at the elderly butler. "How is it I've never seen you in town?"

"I don't go to town." He seemed perplexed by her question. "Why would I? Everything I need is here." He inclined his head. "If you will wait here, I'll see if Miss Daisy is available."

She expected the elderly gentleman to stroll off to speak with Daisy, but he pulled out a cell phone and punched some keys. After a moment, he looked up.

"Miss Daisy will receive you in the kitchen, Mrs. Grant. Apparently meeting in kitchens is your custom."

Suz laughed. "The kitchen is the heart of the home, isn't it?"

"I'm sure you're right. If you'll follow me, please."

"Thank you."

"Hi, Suz!" Daisy exclaimed, coming to greet her in a huge kitchen that was as gray as the weather outside. "Come in and have a seat."

Suz approached cautiously, wondering if Robert Donovan would pop out from somewhere in the cavernous kitchen and give her a spooking she wasn't likely to forget. Suz shivered. Barnabas Collins of Dark Shadows fame was probably inclined to stop by for a late-night Bloody Mary in this place. "Your home is uh, lovely, Daisy."

Daisy waved her to a high-backed chair. Suz sat down stiffly in the even stiffer chair, and Daisy put a cup of tea in front of her that the butler brewed up in some kind of fancy machine. "You're saying it to be polite. It's nothing like the Hanging H."

That was true. Suz felt a little sick thinking about the decor of the Hanging H changing to a *Dark Shadows* castle. "Daisy, listen, I've been thinking."

Daisy sat down across from her, crossed her stiletto-booted legs. "I've been thinking, too. We're going to have to do something."

"Do something?"

Daisy nodded. "Do something to stop my father from taking over Bridesmaids Creek."

Chapter Seventeen

Suz glanced around, wondered if she'd heard the bad girl of Bridesmaids Creek correctly. "Excuse me? Stop your father from gobbling up our town? Isn't that what the goal has been for years?"

Daisy nodded. "Two things make me believe that isn't the right course for our family tree."

"Go on," Suz said, amazed by this turn of events. "I'm hanging on your every word."

"First of all, the luster went out of the thing for me when Dad took over your place."

"I can't say the moment held a lot of luster for me, either."

"You recall I'd just returned from Branch's compound. I've been thinking through everything he taught me, and honestly, I don't think the acquisitive path we're on is a path he'd totally endorse."

Suz swallowed. "I've said it before, I'm going to have to meet this paragon."

Daisy laughed. "You won't unless you go to Montana. I'd go back myself, except you need me right now."

"Yes, I do," Suz said. "I absolutely do."

"And I need you to convince my father that what he's doing isn't the proper path for our lineage," Daisy said.

"Oh, wow, I'm pretty sure— No, that's probably not something I can help you with, Daisy. Sorry."

"He does own your property," Daisy reminded her.

"That's kind of what makes it hard for me to be the one to convince him."

"You're perfect," Daisy said. "And it's very, very important that you do this, Suz."

"Why is this so important to you?" Suz was completely flummoxed by the direction of the conversation.

Daisy leaned close, glanced around, Suz supposed, to make certain Barnabas—er, Robert—wasn't lurking about listening to her scheming. "Dad's ticker just isn't cut out for high-speed wheeling and dealing," Daisy explained. "I'd like my father around to see my grand-children one day. And he won't if he keeps being a wheeler-dealer. Do you know he just bought land in Australia?" Daisy demanded. "Where does it stop?"

"Australia? Why Australia?"

"He got a good deal on something. Along with an office building." Daisy shrugged. "He's looking at something in Dubai now, with a consortium of finan-ciers— Oh, never mind. The only business we should discuss is BC business. I want my father to slow down. And I don't want him taking over your farm."

"He already did," Suz said hollowly. "Cisco and I are hoping you're already looking for a new place for us."

"Let's not lose hope yet. You convince my father, and we'll all be happy."

"We have a month, Daisy. Right after the new year, we have to be out. I think Mackenzie's already lined up movers for her and Justin and the four babies."

Daisy rang a small bell. The butler reappeared like a phantom.

"Yes, miss?"

"Barclay, could you please make us a small tray? Ms. Grant and I would like to move to the garden."

That sounded cold. The snow was coming down fiercely. "I can't stay—"

Daisy waved her to follow. "Stay another half hour. We have a lot to discuss."

She led her into an enclosed, heated porch that looked out on a garden that was breathtaking, even in winter. Suz could only imagine how beautiful it would be in the spring. Lavish gardens inside gardens surrounded amazing statues and ornaments that were now snow-topped. A few bird feeders hung about, hosting cardinals, chickadees, titmice and some other birds Suz didn't have time to catalog. She sat in a padded chintz armchair near the huge bowed-out bay window. "This is lovely, Daisy."

Daisy sat across from her, and a moment later, Barclay came in with a tea tray and two plates of cucumber finger sandwiches and assorted cookies. "Thank you, Barclay."

He nodded and left, and Daisy hopped up to make certain the door was closed behind him. "I didn't want him to overhear. He's been with me since I was a baby, and I know I can trust him, but still, anyone can have a moment of indiscretion."

Suz couldn't have been more poleaxed if Santa had appeared right in the room with them. She bit into the most delicious cucumber sandwich she'd ever eaten, to keep herself from saying, *Who are you? Why have you changed so much?*

"Here's what I think we should do," Daisy said. "I

believe you should sue my father to get your land, home and business back."

"*Sue* your father?" Suz put the sandwich down. "A lawsuit? How can we sue if the foreclosure's already gone through? And anyway, it's not like we can pay."

"And then," Daisy said, totally ignoring her, "I think we should move the Haunted H."

Suz waited, not sure where Daisy was going with that.

"If the Haunted H runs its business elsewhere, it's not attached to your property, you see. You made it all too easy to acquire, because it was all in the same place. Under one ownership, one business."

"Where would we move it?"

Daisy smiled. "My idea is we move it to Bridesmaids Creek, right on the banks. We're famous for our creek, and that's where our magic is. It makes sense to have our town's largest business on our best town asset, don't you think?"

Suz sat quietly, thinking. "I guess he didn't buy the actual Haunted H."

"No, he didn't, because you're the Haunted H. You can call it anything you like, but you and Mackenzie and your parents claim the key to that enterprise. No one else knows how to run a haunted house amusement park for families and kiddies."

"I just don't get why you're so determined to help me," Suz said, honestly confused.

"I told you, I learned a lot in Montana. But if you want the bottom-line facts, I want friends just as much as the next person does. I want to belong here in Bridesmaids Creek. I love it here." She looked out the window at the gently falling snow. "And while I'm being honest, there's one more reason."

Daisy had a heckuva list for Santa Claus going already. "Which is?"

"I haven't given up on my own magic one day," Daisy said softly, turning her gaze to Suz's. "And I figure the only way the magic ever works for me is that I make up for all the harm I did to the heart and soul of Bridesmaids Creek. They said good gets good," Daisy said, "and I'm not claiming I'm good—not yet—but I'm sure as heck going to give being good my very best shot."

Suz smiled. "We'll work this out together."

"Excellent. Because I'm relying on you to change my father's heart," Daisy said, and Suz hoped that even Robert Donovan's stone-cold heart might be changed— this time for good.

UPON FURTHER REFLECTION, Suz knew Daisy was right. "You could liken it to cutting off the head of the snake, I suppose," she told Cisco as they drove to meet Robert at Bridesmaids Creek. She'd wanted the meeting on neutral ground, and this was as neutral as it could get.

If anything was neutral in Bridesmaids Creek.

"Hello, Robert," she said to Mr. Donovan when they met at the usual finish line for Bridesmaids Creek swims. "Thank you for coming."

"I'm quite busy, so we need to make this meeting fast." Robert glared at Cisco. "I suppose you need to let your woman speak for you."

"Yes, I do," Cisco said cheerfully. "And she'll do a damn fine job of it. I'm just going to sit over here and watch the fireworks." He sat himself on a wooden bench, looking as if he couldn't be more relaxed.

"Mr. Donovan," Suz said, "you've gone back on your word you gave to Jade Harper, and Bridesmaids Creek. You're not supposed to be acquiring any part of BC anymore, especially not for your own gain. That was your promise, and in return, Jade would let you see your grandchildren."

Robert shrugged. "I have my own daughter to think of."

"And Ty Spurlock is your son. You're hurting him and your grandchildren by doing this. And the only reason you're doing it is plain old-fashioned greed."

"I can't seem to help myself," Robert said.

Suz nodded. "I'm going to help you."

He beetled his brows. "How?"

"Your daughter has suggested that my sister and I sue you to get our ranch back. But I don't think I have to do that. I think you'll agree to sell it back to Mackenzie and me for one dollar."

Robert sucked in his cheeks. "Young lady, I'd be out a hefty sum."

"You'll want to do it for the good of Bridesmaids Creek." Suz glanced around. "I'm meeting with the town council to pitch the idea of moving our haunted house and Santa's village right here. That's also Daisy's idea."

Robert looked as if he couldn't believe—and didn't like—what he was hearing. "You can't do that. I'm going to buy up all this land."

"Actually, you're not. According to Cosette and Jane Chatham, this is land that's considered Bridesmaids Creek's. Which means you can't purchase it. It's to be used for the good of all in the town. And the town believes that our prime tourist attraction, the haunted house, would be best situated on one of our most revered and beautiful sites." Suz looked around. "I don't know why I never thought of it before. It'll be perfect here."

Robert shook his head. "I'll stop you."

"You won't, because your daughter wants you to change. And you'll do whatever Daisy wants," Suz said. "Daisy's not happy with your behavior, and I'm pretty sure her father wants her to be proud of him."

He stared at her silently.

"Mr. Donovan, Daisy is trying very hard to turn over a new leaf. She wants a do-over in her life. In fact," Suz continued, "Daisy loves Bridesmaids Creek. And she wants to enjoy a lot of the wonderful things we have here. Friendships, charm, local beauty." She looked at Robert narrowly. "Why are you so bent on destroying the wonderful thing that is Bridesmaids Creek? Is your soul so hard that your grandchildren, your newfound son and your daughter don't even matter to you?"

Donovan glanced at Cisco, receiving a shrug and a grin in return. "Now, look here—"

"Here's the thing. Daisy's offered to pay for our legal fees to fight you in court," Suz said softly. "From her very own trust fund, Daisy wants to do good. So all I can say to you is you ought to be very proud of your daughter, Mr. Donovan. Because without any help from you at all, Daisy is making a real effort to become one of us."

He glared at her a moment longer, then headed off to the stretch Hummer that was waiting for him. The Hummer pulled away silently after Robert got in, and Suz felt strengthened when Cisco put his arms around her.

"That was awesome. Did I ever tell you that I fell for you in the very beginning, the first time I ever met you—and you totally sealed the deal when you put your little hands on your hips and told me I wasn't going to be Frog anymore? That you were renaming me Cisco?" He smiled down at her. "I thought any little lady with that much sass had my name on her."

"You mean *has* my name on you."

"Exactly what I meant." He kissed her, and Suz leaned into his body, loving how he was always there for her. "Let's go home and relieve Betty from babysitting duty. I have a yen to see my little ladies and hold them tight," Cisco said.

"Sounds good to me."

They started to walk toward their truck—then Cisco suddenly turned. "Hang on a second."

"What is it?"

Cisco listened a second more. "Come on out, Sam."

Sam filtered into the clearing, and Cisco laughed. "You were there the whole time, weren't you?"

"Just in case you needed me." Sam kissed Suz on the cheek, high-fived Cisco. "I don't think I'm going to need to camp here anymore. Listening to Suz gave me faith that life in BC is about to change for the better very soon."

"We're all about letting bygones be bygones in BC," Cisco said. "Come on. We'll give you a ride back to the bunkhouse. You're going to love sleeping in a real bed."

Suz smiled happily. Sam wasn't the only man who was going to love sleeping in a real bed. It was time to move the babies to a nearby crib, and hold her husband in her arms—forever.

"Now we figure out how to save Daisy," Suz said after they'd checked in on the babies. Fed them, loved on them—and then asked doting Aunt Mackenzie and Uncle Justin to watch them for a while.

Cisco hesitated. "Daisy?"

"She's the base we're building our case on. And to save her, we have to give her what she wants and needs the most. Otherwise, her father may be able to turn her back."

He escorted his wife to their truck. "So where are we going?"

"We're going to hunt up Daisy's gang. They're the ones who can help."

"I don't know." He was doubtful as he helped her in. They left the ranch, and drove into town as they both pondered the situation. "Have Daisy's gang ever been helpful?"

"We've got to try. They're the only ones who are in love with Daisy. One of them has to be her handsome prince."

"What do we do about Squint?"

"Squint left Montana, took himself to parts unknown. We may never see him in BC again. We don't have time to wait on him to save Daisy."

Cisco wasn't certain about leaving his buddy out of this, but Suz had been right about everything else so far. He pulled the truck up in front of the gang's lair, now holed up in Cosette's old office. The *Madame Matchmaker's Premiere Matchmaking Services* sign still scrolled across the window, but now a white sign was taped on the door.

The Gang's All Here Premiere Dating Services read the sign.

This change in Bridesmaids Creek felt very wrong.

"It's just temporary," Dig said, noticing him and Suz

staring at the taped placard. "We've ordered a new sign for the front window, and a hanging shingle that's nice and fancy."

Cisco glanced at Suz, who shrugged. They followed Dig inside. Cosette's delicate furniture was covered with sheets. One wall now had black moiré wallpaper going up on it—elegant, in a "Donovan's influence can be felt here, gray and dark" kind of way. Leather seats had been brought in, low-slung and masculine, and Cisco thought he smelled cigar smoke.

"Is that a cigar bar?" he demanded.

"Among other things," Red said. "We're just getting started with it, but yeah, the humidor should come in next week."

"Holy Christmas. How'd you get this setup past the committee?" Cisco couldn't believe how changed the space was. There were even wrought-iron chandeliers hanging from the ceiling, and a couple of fancy sconces around a huge mirror where the leather-wrapped cigar bar would go.

"We didn't," Clint said. "We're putting it in, then selling them on the idea."

"It's not half-bad," Suz said quickly.

"The town pillars are going to throw a fit," Cisco said.

"Be positive, Cisco," Suz said, and he instantly got the script.

"I have to say I admire your business, er, sense," he said.

"Wish you'd thought of it, huh?" Carson asked.

"Clearly my mind doesn't work this way." Suz smiled at him, and Cisco decided to keep the greater mission in mind. "So, have you fellows got a second?"

"Sure. Have a seat," Gabriel said, and he and Suz took a seat—even though in his heart, Cisco thought it felt wrong. This was Cosette's place—it wasn't fair or right that she was no longer in here, holding court in her pink-frosted fairy-tale world.

"So we were wondering," Cisco said, "if you guys have realized that Daisy is the key to your happiness."

They stared at him, dumbfounded.

"Well, yeah," Carson said, "but it was hard as hell getting Squint out of the picture, dude. She's not ours now—but she's not his, either."

"What we mean," Suz said, and Cisco grinned as he recognized the soft touch was about to be applied, "is that we think there's been an error, a Bridesmaids Creek error. Squint was never the one who was meant for Daisy."

Suz had their rapt attention. Cisco leaned back in the leather seat, accepted a cigar from Dig. It was going to be something to celebrate just to watch his love work her magic.

"We figure it has to be one of you," Suz continued. "Maybe. I mean, it makes sense, right?"

"What about him?" Red asked, jerking his head toward Cisco.

"Oh, that was the Bridesmaids Creek error," Suz said.

"Our legends have never been wrong," Clint said. "There has never been a misfire in Bridesmaids Creek, except for your sister Mackenzie's first marriage."

"There's that," Suz said. "We Hawthorne women might be a little hard for magic to work on."

Cisco didn't agree with that. As far as he was concerned, Suz was the most magical woman he'd ever met—but he kept his mouth busy with the cigar, happily silent and relaxing, listening to the best yarn he'd ever heard told in Bridesmaids Creek unfold.

"The thing is," Suz said, "we realized the magic had been misplaced."

Cisco's gaze—along with the five Daisy devotees—was riveted on Suz. This was a new tack, and he was anxious to hear more.

"See that Saint Michael medal Cisco always wears?"

They nodded, and Cisco automatically felt for the chain keeping the medal secure around his neck. If he had magic, it was this. It had kept him safe in Afghanistan—it was probably protecting him now.

"John Squint Mathison gave Cisco that medal, after they graduated BUD/S, and before they went to Afghanistan," Suz said. "There was a Saint Michael charm buried in Ty Spurlock's house, that was left to him by his mother. Sam has one, and Squint has one. But the medal that Cisco wears was switched with Squint's one day when they were at training, and they never switched back. Squint had got his when he was a kid, trawling along behind the traveling rodeo. It was given to him by a peddler who said it would always protect him."

The men waited, dumbfounded and spellbound.

"The Bridesmaids Creek magic was misplaced because Cisco is wearing Squint's medallion," Suz finished. "The magic got confused. Daisy was never in love with Cisco. And she admitted that to me. Even she was confused. She said she'd only wanted Cisco because I'd wanted him," Suz said, and Cisco said, "Let's be careful of my ego here."

Suz grinned at him, and Cisco puffed contentedly

on his cigar, not bothered in the least, rather enjoying his starring role in the story.

"That's what happened. When Daisy realized she'd never been in love with Cisco—after her trip to Montana—she figured she needed a different prince."

Five Daisy fans sat up, looking very hopeful.

"But the problem is," Suz continued, "she's gone again."

"Gone where?" Gabriel asked.

"Back to Montana."

Carson gasped. "Not back to that Branch character! He got her so turned around we hardly recognized her!"

"She was totally changed," Clint agreed. "We have to stop her. When did she leave?"

"About two hours ago," Suz said innocently.

"You're sure about this magic stuff not working? Misfiring?" Dig asked, clearly not wanting to suffer another disappointment.

"Cosette and Jane Chatham are the ones who helped me figure it out." Suz sent them her best *what-are-you-waiting-for* innocent look. "They're never wrong, you know."

"Well, they were wrong about Mackenzie once—" Clint began, but Suz said, "If you hurry, you can still catch her at the state line. Just be warned, Daisy has her heart set on her own day of Bridesmaids Creek magic—now that she knows that the three races were totally ineligible. Because of the magic misfire," Suz said.

"Yeah," Gabriel said thoughtfully. "Can I see that medal for a second, Cisco?"

Dutifully he held it up. The men gazed at it with some reverence.

"You really think it saved your life?" Red asked.

"I know it did." Cisco nodded, certain on that point.

"Even though it's Squint's?"

"I don't really question the supernatural and the angels and saints in my life," Cisco said. "But I'm pretty sure they don't make mistakes, either."

"That's good enough for me. I'm ready for a road trip," Gabriel said.

"I'm ready to bring our girl home," Red agreed.

"Can you lock up, close the door behind you when you've finished your cigar?" Carson asked.

"Sure." Cisco smiled. "Happy hunting, fellows."

The men tore out of there like they couldn't let one more mile get between them and Daisy.

"My love," he said, pulling Suz into his lap, "I believe you've been taking lessons from Cosette."

Suz snuggled into his neck. "I'm glad you think so. For a minute there, I wondered if I was overdoing it."

He laughed, delighted with his bride. "You didn't overdo it in the least. If anything, you may have changed the destiny of Bridesmaids Creek. Once they bring Daisy back, we'll put her in charge of the haunted house plans."

"Robert won't dare disappoint Daisy." Suz kissed him. "It's a pretty good plan you thought up. If I didn't know better, I'd say you were born and raised in BC, my prince."

"I came late to the party, but I'm learning fast." He buried his face against Suz's neck, inhaling her fragrance and warm body scent that was hers alone. "You're the most amazing woman I ever met, and I can't imagine my life without you. We just have one small problem left."

Suz gazed down into his eyes. "Whatever it is, we

can solve it together. That's one thing I learned about us—we're a great team."

"Yes, we are. But I believe we promised our town a real wedding. A Bridesmaids Creek wedding."

She smiled. "You're right. We did."

"How does Christmas Eve sound to you?"

"Lovely. And then our first Christmas morning with the babies. Nothing would make me happier, Cisco."

Cisco grinned, tossed his cigar into the proper cigar disposal the gang had thoughtfully supplied for their future customers. Picked up his bride, carried her out the door and locked it behind them. "We're going to have to figure out a way to get this place back into Cosette's charming possession. We can't have a dating service replacing our resident matchmaker."

Suz laughed as he carried her to the truck. "Everything always works out in Bridesmaids Creek eventually. Haven't you noticed?"

"Indeed I have." And he was thankful for that, because in a town where even the smallest story was a really tall tale, magic was very, very important.

He was living proof that even a frog could get the small-town princess, and the happiest, most magical fairy tale ending of all.

Epilogue

Christmas Eve day

"Don't think I don't know exactly what you're doing," Robert Donovan said to Suz as he waited with her under a beautiful rose bower. He looked very dapper in a black bow tie and fancy tux—he'd insisted that if he was going to stand in her father's place at a wedding, he was going to look the part—and held her hand over his arm most delicately, as if fearing he might hurt her. "You bought your house back from me for a dollar and are building your own place on the land I gave up pursuing." His brows rose as she smiled at him. "Then you sent six bachelors who are all in love with my daughter to romance her in Montana!"

Suz couldn't hold back her delighted giggle. "To be fair, I only sent the five musketeers after her. Squint may have already been there. Daisy was determined to go back on her own. But she flew in for the wedding and for Christmas—that should make you very happy."

"Yes, but something about Montana has changed her. Doesn't seem like my Daisy anymore."

"It's hard when your little girl grows up, isn't it?"

"Hmph." He looked embarrassed. "Just focus on your

walk down the aisle, my dear. Your time will come soon enough when your own daughters fly the proverbial coop."

Suz beamed. "Grandchildren are a parents' bonus, if you think about it. Daisy may leave the nest, but you'll get more grandchildren. And I know you have a heart in there you're trying to hide, Robert. I know you adore those little granddaughters."

He hmphed again. "They're growing on me."

"You know what I think? I think a long time ago someone told you that life was hard. That it was tough. So you grew a really tough shell. Like an armadillo," Suz said.

"Are you trying to get on my good side?" Robert asked. "Because if you are, you probably don't want to compare me to one of the world's most unattractive animals."

Suz laughed as the bridal music began to play. "We'll keep working on it."

He patted her hand, not saying anything, readying himself to step forward to give her away.

"You know," Suz said softly, "if one of those six men could win Daisy's heart, you could be standing here one more time giving your own daughter away. You look quite handsome in this role."

He patted her hand again, clutching it in the crook of his arm. "Young lady, have you ever heard that flattery will get you nowhere?"

"Yes. But this is Bridesmaids Creek. We live by different rules."

Mackenzie turned to look at her. "Here we go!"

She sounded so excited that Suz was glad she and Cisco had agreed to have a wedding for all of Bridesmaids Creek to participate in. They began the slow march of the bridal procession, and Suz smiled at her guests as Robert escorted her up the aisle. There was Sheriff McAdams, of course, and his wife, Shirley, and Jane and Ralph Chatham, among others. They held the babies, sharing them with Cisco's parents and brothers, who were seated in a place of honor. Suz had insisted that Cisco invite them, so they could experience Bridesmaids Creek at its finest—because BC was never in better form than when turning out for a wedding.

Much to Cisco's surprise, Suz loved his family, and they seemed very much to return those emotions, not to mention being entirely smitten with their first grandchildren.

Inviting his parents had been just one way she intended to show Cisco that she loved him dearly. And as they liked to say in Bridesmaids Creek, bygones were bygones. The old Suz would have been scared stiff of anything to do with a "minor-minor royal" designation, but family was just family, after all, and Suz loved her husband and her children too much to cheat them of the other side of their family. Nothing was more important than family.

Mackenzie looked so proud as she waited for Robert and Suz to approach the altar—but nobody looked more proud than Cisco.

"You're absolutely beautiful," he told her, and Suz smiled, completely in love. Head over heels in love.

"You're pretty handsome yourself."

Of course he was more than handsome—he was the man she'd adored from afar before she'd ever swam for him. "I love you," she whispered. "And those darling babies you gave me?"

They glanced over at the babies with delight.

"Thank you for them."

"I told you it would be no problem at all," Cisco said, bragging just a little as he kissed her. Of course it was all out of order, he should have kissed her after the ceremony, but the pastor didn't seem to mind a bit. If anything, Suz saw a twinkle in his eyes, and the guests clapped, so everything was just fine. In fact, it was magical. Just another magical, enchanted day in Bridesmaids Creek.

Which was why, after the "I do's" were said, and the kissing enthusiastically done once again, Suz dropped her bouquet right into Daisy Donovan's lap before walking back up the aisle.

"Good aim," Cisco said.

And Suz laughed, because in Bridesmaids Creek, the magic was bound to strike—whether you were looking for it or not.

That was the secret of Bridesmaids Creek—there was always magic in the air.

* * * * *

Daisy's story is next! Watch for
THE COWBOY SEAL'S TRIPLETS,
the final story in Tina Leonard's
BRIDESMAIDS CREEK miniseries.
Coming July 2015,
only from Harlequin American Romance!

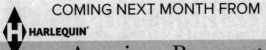

REQUEST YOUR FREE BOOKS!
2 FREE NOVELS PLUS 2 FREE GIFTS!

HARLEQUIN

American ★ Romance®

LOVE, HOME & HAPPINESS

YES! Please send me 2 FREE Harlequin® American Romance® novels and my 2 FREE gifts (gifts are worth about $10). After receiving them, if I don't wish to receive any more books, I can return the shipping statement marked "cancel." If I don't cancel, I will receive 4 brand-new novels every month and be billed just $4.74 per book in the U.S. or $5.24 per book in Canada. That's a savings of at least 14% off the cover price! It's quite a bargain! Shipping and handling is just 50¢ per book in the U.S. and 75¢ per book in Canada.* I understand that accepting the 2 free books and gifts places me under no obligation to buy anything. I can always return a shipment and cancel at any time. Even if I never buy another book, the two free books and gifts are mine to keep forever.

154/354 HDN F4YN

Name _____ (PLEASE PRINT)

Address _____ Apt. #

City _____ State/Prov. _____ Zip/Postal Code

Signature (if under 18, a parent or guardian must sign)

Mail to the **Harlequin® Reader Service:**
IN U.S.A.: P.O. Box 1867, Buffalo, NY 14240-1867
IN CANADA: P.O. Box 609, Fort Erie, Ontario L2A 5X3

Want to try two free books from another line?
Call 1-800-873-8635 or visit www.ReaderService.com.

* Terms and prices subject to change without notice. Prices do not include applicable taxes. Sales tax applicable in N.Y. Canadian residents will be charged applicable taxes. Offer not valid in Quebec. This offer is limited to one order per household. Not valid for current subscribers to Harlequin American Romance books. All orders subject to credit approval. Credit or debit balances in a customer's account(s) may be offset by any other outstanding balance owed by or to the customer. Please allow 4 to 6 weeks for delivery. Offer available while quantities last.

Your Privacy—The Harlequin® Reader Service is committed to protecting your privacy. Our Privacy Policy is available online at www.ReaderService.com or upon request from the Harlequin Reader Service.

We make a portion of our mailing list available to reputable third parties that offer products we believe may interest you. If you prefer that we not exchange your name with third parties, or if you wish to clarify or modify your communication preferences, please visit us at www.ReaderService.com/consumerschoice or write to us at Harlequin Reader Service Preference Service, P.O. Box 9062, Buffalo, NY 14269. Include your complete name and address.

HARI3R

Ryder stood at the pasture fence, his leather dress shoes sinking into the soft dirt. He'd have a chore cleaning them later. At the moment, he didn't care.

When, he absently wondered, was the last time he'd worn a pair of boots? Or ridden a horse, for that matter? The answer came quickly. Five years ago. He'd sworn then and there he'd never set sight on Reckless again.

Recent events had altered the circumstance of his enduring disagreement with his family. Liberty, the one most hurt by their mother's lies, had managed to make peace with both their parents. Not so Ryder. His anger had not dimmed one bit.

Was coming home a mistake? Only time would tell. In any case, he wasn't staying long.

In the pasture, a woman haltered a large black pony and led it slowly toward the gate. Ryder leaned his forearms on the top fence railing. Even at this distance, he could tell two things: the pony was severely lame, and the woman was spectacularly attractive.

The pair was a study in contrast. While the pony hobbled painfully, favoring its front left foot, the woman moved with elegance and grace, her long black hair misbehaving in the mild breeze. She stopped frequently to check on the pony, and when she did, rested her hand affectionately on its sleek neck.

Something about her struck a familiar, but elusive, chord with him. A memory teased at the fringes of his mind, just out of reach.

As he watched, the knots of tension residing in his shoulders relaxed. That was, until she changed direction and headed toward him. Then he immediately perked up, and his senses went on high alert.

"Hi," she said as she approached. "Can I help you?"

She was even prettier up close. Large, dark eyes analyzed him with unapologetic interest from a model-perfect oval face. Her full mouth stretched into a warm smile impossible not to return. The red T-shirt tucked into a pair of well-worn jeans emphasized her long legs and slim waist.

"I'm meeting someone." He didn't add that he was now ten minutes late or that the someone was, in fact, his father.

"Can I show you the way?"

"Thanks. I already know it."

"You've been here before?"

"You…could say that. But it's been a while."

Look for HER RODEO MAN by New York Times bestselling author Cathy McDavid, available March 2015 wherever Harlequin American Romance books and ebooks are sold!